Midwinter Madness

Conscience and cowardice are really the same things. Conscience is the trade-name of the firm.

OSCAR WILDE
The Picture of Dorian Gray

Chapter 1

December 15.   Pre-dawn.

"THE RUSSKI'S waking up!" A deep voice boomed.
Others chimed in.
   " 'Ere, Ivan!"
   "Wakey-wakey, mate!"
   "Give 'im a good-morning kiss!"
   "Good-morning kick!"
   "Leave the bugger alone. Just look at him. His head's
hurting something terrible."
   It did. It hurt so much I didn't care whose were the
voices, where they came from, how they resonated and
clanged like brass tongues in my hollow skull. I almost
didn't care about the stench of tobaccoey breath and

damp wool that was curdling the acids in my stomach. For another minute I did nothing while the floor beneath me jolted and rattled. Then the angle tilted, and I rolled painfully against a line of boots and gun butts. Okay. Dreaming over. Time to chip out of my eggshell and find out where the hell I was.

Opening the first eye, I thought I'd been blinded. The haziest outlines of bodies slowly began to appear. With the help of the second eye I saw why sight was so slow coming. I was in the back of a van scarcely lit by a small portable lantern strapped to the inside handle of the rear door. As for the men themselves, their features were invisible. Right next to my eyes were their dark rubber-soled boots. Looking inch by inch up past the two rows of French workingmen's *bleus de travail* and fishermen's sweaters buttoned along the left shoulder, I stopped, confused, at the heads. No faces—only brown woolen face masks up to their foreheads. Brown woolen caps on their heads. Like Palestinian shock troops clumsily disguised as Frenchmen . . . or the other way around.

On second thought, with their peasant outfits and masks, they looked less like cosmopolitan guerrillas than a contingent from the Thirty Years' War, strayed into the wrong century.

I tried to say something, but managed only a grunt. Speech could wait.

"*Merde!*" I heard a voice say.

"Hey, English only. Orders. Stick to 'em, 'less you lost the taste for bread."

Ah! It was coming back. That was "the sergeant-major" speaking, a Marine Michael Caine, the guy with the cropped hair and granite shoulders. I'd seen him before somewhere—where? Why did he speak in that mad mixture of Guernsey twang, Midlands cockney and word-for-word translations of Parisian underworld argot? Where had I met him? Met him! Christ, he'd mugged me in . . . Beaumont. Right. We were in France. In Normandy, the Cotentin peninsula, somewhere near Cherbourg. At least we had been when I was last conscious. And where the hell was my friend Pierre Denis now?

I started to put the question to the sergeant-major.

"*Écrase!*" he yelled from up front on the right, cradling a submachine gun. He didn't mind disobeying his own orders about speaking English, but then he had his very own lingo, neither French nor English. "It's me that pisses on the wall round here, Bolcho," he told me. "Don't try shitting on me, *hein?*"

"Okay, you're the boss," I mumbled.

A minute passed, a minute of stopping and starting. I noticed that rain had begun to drum on the roof of the van.

"Got a fag?" said a (genuine) Cockney voice. "Ta!"

A man near my feet caught the pack tossed by another man opposite. He inserted a cigarette through woolen lips and lit the end, swearing softly.

"English bloody cigarettes!" mocked the sergeant-major. "Herring skin. *Merde!*"

"You been too long in this bloody country," said a voice. "Ruins your palate, France, that's what it does."

"Belt up, Jack," said another voice, the very deep one, definitely Channel Islands. "I saw you smoke a Gauloise this morning."

"No names. You all got numbers. Use 'em," barked the sergeant-major.

"Don't put sticks in the fuckin' wheels, eh, *Number Eight!*" the Cockney voice shot back, teasing.

3

Laughter.

I had a sudden idea I'd woken up onstage during the performance of an audience-participation drama in some café-theater or upstairs room off-Off-Broadway.

"Right!" announced the sergeant-major, with sudden authority. "Questions? Last chance."

"Nah!"

"Yeah. How much time we got to get away?"

"None at all if we run out of luck. Depends on their radio contacts. But the *flics* won't get worried if the convoy's a couple of minutes late."

"Two bloody minutes! That all we got?"

"Right. So move when I tell you. More?"

"I got one. What're we going to do with this bugger?" A kick to my ribs made sure everyone understood who was being referred to.

"Knock 'im off," said a voice, muffled.

"That's the boss's business," said the sergeant-major, failing to shed light on a problem that interested me greatly. I would have tried a supplementary question myself but a voice interrupted.

"What's 'e along with us for anyway?"

"Hostage, Number Two. Ivan here's our hostage. Except if you do what you've been ordered to we won't need one, will we?"

"Still and all, we couldn't have left him back there. Two against one and all."

"Okay. That'll do it," the sergeant-major snapped.

But my mind wasn't functioning. I couldn't piece together all these scrappy bits of information.

"No more questions? Right." The sergeant-major paused, daring a word from the others. None came. "Okay. It's six-thirty-five. De-bus in . . . four minutes." He issued orders in the accent of movie parade-ground

4

sergeants. It wouldn't have been any good whispering though; the rain was now beating on the roof like a flock of demented woodpeckers.

"And Bolcho!" the sergeant-major added sharply. "Stay here. Right where you are. Stick your ass down, don't ask questions, don't move a muscle."

"*Banco!*" I said, though I wasn't sure I was capable of moving muscles, or had any left worth moving.

Someone tittered.

There was a distinct feeling in the stale air of an operation irrevocably under way, of the action—finally —imminent; that tense nervous atmosphere when troops are working themselves up to suppressing their natural cowardice while still thinking, Are these my last thoughts? My last moments? Surely I didn't mean to get myself in this situation? What's everyone else doing out there, at peace with the world, not thinking of me, not knowing or caring that I'm going to die . . . ?

It's the same every time. Only the very battle-hardened, the guys who get promoted to sergeant-major, think about plans and positions and synchronizing watches now.

But *what* action? What was going on? I wished my head were clearer.

Or did I? There was this feeling of danger, of horror, a feeling I had no wish to face with clarity. The earlier urge to recall the events that had led to my being here in the van began to grow faint in my mind. But it was no use. Try as I would, fragments of memory kept assaulting me. My head hurt more than ever. The pain grew steadily as consciousness beat back the oblivion that my innate cowardice had tried to reimpose.

Then an image appeared in my brain. An image of an airport, then another of a small bright orange plane

5

. . . streaked with water, a rainy morning. England. Oh God . . . yes, that was when I believed I was off to fight another battle. Amanda's father. I couldn't stop it. It was all coming back.

Chapter 2

December 13. 10:30 A.M.

AMANDA HAD seen me off at Southampton with tears in her eyes. Tears or just rainspots on my airplane window, it was hard to tell. As I fumbled with my safety belt, I watched her tall figure in a beige trenchcoat and mottled headscarf, sheltering in the doorway of a whitewashed shed, wave, turn, then disappear. The plane, a ten-seat Islander bound for Guernsey, the second largest of the Channel Islands, began to taxi. Then in a sudden rush it roared down the rainsoaked runway, hydroplaning, till the nose lifted clear of the water and we were airborne. I was the only passenger.

Good-by Amanda.

My Amanda!

I'd met her half a year before, at a dinner party. She in a bitchy post-divorce mood; I just as crabby. About what I don't remember. We got on well together. We went on to a night club. (She was a creature of "swinging London," despite a first-class degree in philosophy from London University.) As a lover she was witty, experienced, yet—touchingly I thought at first—a bit of a fraud. She'd needed several stiff drinks to overcome an innate middle-class puritanism which she tried to hide but which came over her with a compulsive shudder when the consciousness of being naked with a man could no longer be repressed. Her best moments came after boozy lunches when she could keep most of her clothes on and pretend to herself it was just horseplay behind the tennis courts. I would take her back to my Kensington apartment where she would pretend to be drunk, sleepy, stretch out on the floor, half-undress, showing me glimpses of underwear, push me away, moan; grab my hand and thrust it between her legs, cry "no! no!" and succumb. Almost a routine.

She began to relax with me, but after a struggle. Maybe I kept on only because it was a struggle, because I flattered myself that smooth-talking Dr. Gull—he and his cultivated cosmopolitan bedside manner—was ridding her of harmful British inhibitions . . . .

So successfully that now she was pregnant.

I sometimes wonder if it wasn't the total lack of privacy during my youth in pre-war Moscow, the total lack of any opportunity to make love as instinct dictated, that led me into chronic satyriasis . . . Excuses! It couldn't have been any easier at Amanda's snobbish boarding school . . . .

A sudden jolt brought me back to the reality of flying

8

in rough weather inside this taxi with wings. In fact the storm clouds we had encountered over the Channel were proving to be mere omens of what was coming up now. The pilot, a fair-haired man scarcely out of his teens, succeeded in dropping us down safely at Maupertus, on the north coast of the Cotentin peninsula. But from the start of our quarter-hour stopover the rain began to batter the plate-glass windows of Cherbourg's neat little airport as if the Good Lord were trying to wash it free from sin. I stirred some sugar into a centimeter of bitter coffee in a chipped green cup and stared out at the smudged gray-green fields beyond the tarmac. It was touch and go, the young pilot told us, whether we would be able to take off again. All the same he was anxious to leave.

"Don't want to get stuck here, do we?" he said with a wink in my direction. He stubbed out a Craven A, an odd cigarette, because it has a false cork tip. "Back to Blighty or bust!"

From one so young! Hadn't he heard of United Europe? I smiled weakly. I'd have preferred France to Guernsey any day, and especially today.

He was chatty. I didn't like that. I never like nervous pilots.

"Going over for business, are you?"

I nodded. "That's about it."

"Salesman, are you?"

"Not exactly. More of an escape artist."

"Oh really? I say, tell me about it. Sounds fascinating."

"It was a joke," I said sourly. "I'm an interpreter. I'm going to Guernsey to interpret."

"That still sounds fascinating," the pilot said, unabashed. But he had in fact lost interest. Fortunately the desultory dialog was interrupted by a young French couple who came to our table and began to gabble at the pilot about the terrible storm, and was it safe for them to get on the flight, the wife being in a . . . "delicate state."

The pilot's own confidence grew as he listened to their alarmed chatter. "Can't understand French myself," he said cheerfully to me when the couple had finished. "Not at that speed. Maybe you can tell them. It's off we go. Blighty or bust! Come on!"

So we struggled up once more; up and into a mass of swirling vapor like steam from a giant bain-marie. The orange paintwork of our tiny Aurigny Air Services plane streamed zigzagging droplets as it lurched and bounced above the cow pastures, over the Cap de Flamanville and out across the sea again. In the bottom left corner of my window the rain bunched in a throbbing ball, sending out streaks like cardiogram readings of a heart attack.

The new passengers had taken the seat behind me. The woman was in an advanced stage of pregnancy all right, with a belly that bulged hugely. She held her husband's right hand very tightly in both of her own. Her eyes were filled with pure love and pure panic.

She was an uncomfortable reminder of Amanda's (and my) predicament. Thank God Amanda had stayed in England. What a foursome of passengers we would have made, like an abortion charter . . . . The plane dropped a sudden two hundred feet. The woman behind me was sick and missed the bag. I stared out of the rain-smeared window and wondered how it would be to just step out into those soft enveloping clouds and solve our problem that way . . . .

Then a thought distracted me.

The approach to Guernsey had spontaneously recalled the miscellaneous information that Victor Hugo, the French poet, had spent two miserable decades of exile in the Channel Islands. He called them "bits of France fallen into the sea and snatched up by England."

Today the wind was enough to blow them back to the rocky French coast again.

The plane sagged, swung, was sucked up again.

Guernsey itself, where Hugo had spent most of his exile, was invisible now behind the mist. I tried to deduce how close we were getting by looking at the bank of instruments I could almost touch from my seat behind the pilot, but without success. Every time I thought I had a reading, the dexterous young man at the controls hit a switch and needles began to oscillate, figures to whirl like lemons in a fruit machine. What the hell, I was probably assessing our altitude from the radio frequency and the kilometers from the fuel gauge.

The plane lurched yet again, and a whole array of needles plummeted to zero. The pilot wrestled with the joystick to keep us on an even keel. The woman screamed. But suddenly a string of black rocks with white frills flickered into view for a second down below through a gap in the clouds. We were there! Almost. The islands of Herm and Jethou made a sudden, though momentary, appearance. Sark was somewhere to our left, nowhere to be seen. Seconds later a wet, white St. Peter Port, with its flat gray castle on the harbor wall, rose to meet us, and finally we dipped clear of the seething vapor. The plane veered left, away from the town and the gasoline storage tanks on the flatlands of St. Sampson, and flew for another minute over densely huddled villas and greenhouses before a shiny asphalt runway trimmed with yellow Christmas-tree lights gave the wheels a solid thump. We hopped on down, playing ducks and drakes, then slowed and turned toward the airport bungalows.

"From the air it looks just like the old city of Algiers, Vladimir, quite beautiful," Amanda had said. "Castle Cornet's just like a corsair fort." Her accuracy as far as Guernsey's capital was concerned boded ill for my meeting with her father. "Acres and acres of greenhouses, like a phosphorescent sea. Guernsey was called Greneze, you know, darling. It means the Green Isle. You'll love it."

But I didn't. On first impression it was a gray suburbia whose island charm began and ended at its rocky fringe.

AFTER I'D drunk two pints of Pony beer tasting of real hops in one of St. Peter Port's olde worlde pubs, and once the sky had begun to clear in the early afternoon, giving me a chance to walk about, Guernsey began to have charm.

All the same I cursed the conference that had brought me here. When the Guernsey tomato exporters first called me in to help them hard-sell a group of Soviet Prodexport delegates, Amanda had immediately seized the chance.

"Now you can't put off seeing daddy any longer, Vladimir!"

I had indeed never met Godfrey Mackeson-Beadle. He rarely forsook his tax haven, and "meeting the family" has never been a prominent part of my sybaritic life. Besides, it was a fair bet that the old boy never envisioned as his son-in-law a forty-plus ex-Soviet defector and international interpreter with an irregular lifestyle.

Any more than I saw him as a father-in-law. Him or anyone else. Marriage was what Amanda, not I, saw at the end of the tunnel. She refused an abortion, point-blank. She was probably prepared to have the child alone if she had to. But she wasn't giving up on me without a struggle. That was why the tomato confer-ence was so desperately badly timed. It introduced me to her dad, two members of Amanda's expanding family who, according to her, "really should get to know each other." But I'd accepted the interpreting job and now I was here. I might as well make the best of it. I looked back up at the city and its narrow hilly streets. From beside the harbor I could see a grandiose covered mar-ket and, farther up, the tall flat façade of Victor Hugo's Hauteville House. The impression of all this from below was predominantly white, with glimpses here and there of carved balconies. Perhaps it was a bit like Algiers after all, or Gibraltar might be a closer comparison. Or Bexhill-on-Sea. Somehow we English manage to stamp our outposts, however exotic the setting, with that all-too-exportable tattiness of south coast resorts.

At half past two I met the tomato exporters and the Soviet delegates from Prodexport. It was obvious in ten minutes, to all of us, that the Russians had no intention of importing Channel Island tomatoes. They'd already done what they came for during their morning tour of the greenhouses, namely, pick up technical information for use back home. They'd taken their notes, pocketed the literature and were now merely going through the formalities. The deal-that-never-was broke down after two hours of barely disguised pretense, and with frozen smiles one and all thanked me for my work. I had a quiet word with the exporters' secretary to make sure she knew where to send my check and walked out a free man, the only non-Soviet to do well out of the fiasco.

It was a quarter to five and darkening when I plucked up courage and opened the glass door of an oilskin-yellow telephone booth to dial a number that Amanda had impatiently forced me to commit to memory. A thin female voice answered, telling me that Mr. Mackeson-Beadle had unfortunately stepped out for a moment. But he was expecting me, and it would only take a few moments to walk from the center of town to Greenacres. The directions, obviously given by someone who had never walked from the center of town as far as Greenacres, convinced me I'd been right to take note of the taxi stand beside the town church.

As a result I quickly found myself in a taxi winding up a succession of narrow lanes between high stone walls to the posh end of town and out toward Fort George, the old headquarters of the Guernsey militia. The driver, otherwise taciturn, told me angrily when the fort came in sight that it was now a millionaires' mini-suburb; the concession had been given to private speculators by the Deputies against the signed wishes of fifteen thousand islanders.

"Bloody English," he muttered at the end. "Think they own the bloody place."

"I thought they did," I said.

He glared at me, as if to say it was just as well I wasn't English, looked away, then back at me, not quite sure whether I was or not.

But I am! I have a British passport, even if I was born and bred in Moscow. That document, precious to me if anathema to the taxi driver, was snug in my inside pocket. Is it those high Slav cheekbones of mine, perhaps, that give the impression of foreignness?

He turned his small, square Guernesiais face to the

front and drove on a shade more recklessly. The driver of a green bus, squat and short to negotiate the narrow winding lanes of the island, made a gesture with two fingers as we cut in at a crossroads.

But we arrived. Outside the villa gate I paid off my chauffeur with one of the purple five-pound notes that sport on one side a view of the Town Church and on the other three coy and feathery lions, the island's badge. The smaller notes I got back, with an olive-green picture of Castle Cornet in place of the church, so encouraged the impression of playing with funny money that I hugely overtipped him. This confirmed him in his impression that I wasn't, after all, English. He forced a smile.

The taxi drove off happily, leaving me to push open a black on flaking white wooden gate with the name *Greenacres* stenciled on it, and walk up a crazy paving path. On each side the small damp garden smelled richly after the rain. I stood in front of the door.

A real bellpull—and nothing electric about it—announced my presence.

A maid, wearing the uniform of a thirties drawing-room comedy, opened the door.

"Mr. Gull?"

I recognized the thin voice.

"Yes. Is Mr. Mackeson-Beadle back?"

"I believe so, sir. If you would step this way."

I followed the demure domestic into a large square hall with a dark parquet floor and heavy Victorian furniture, then to the right, through to a kind of conservatory-cum-parlor with a chintz sofa and dead tomato plants along the window sill.

"If you'd care to wait here, sir."

"Chambers!" A voice boomed while the maid was

still backing her way out. "Is that Gull? If it is, show him up, will you?"

So the procession set off again, up a curved brown-painted staircase. When I reached the top, the maid was already scurrying off, and I was left alone to confront my father-in-law-to-be, Godfrey Mackeson-Beadle.

He was not a large man, despite the voice which was resonant in a loud upper-class way. More like a caricature-colonel, with a small gray mustache, florid face and stocky frame loosely hung with Harris tweed. He was smiling.

"Good journey? Good show! Delighted to meet you. Amanda's told me all about you and all that."

He turned on his heel without shaking hands. I was used to this English trait by now, having been a British citizen since . . . good God, since as far back as 1956, when I "defected," as the Foreign Office people put it . . .

"Time for a glass of something? Yes, it's getting on. Usual things. What'll it be?"

He directed these remarks back over his shoulder as he led me into a drawingroom one floor up from the entrance at the front of the house; but because of the slope of the land it gave directly out onto a spacious lawn exuding that damp depressing exhalation of English gardens in midwinter.

Three small hissing logs struggled to catch fire in a grate boxed by ocher tiles.

"Don't see so many people since Mousie died. Of course I'm still you might say active in local affairs. Still do some politicking. But things aren't the same as they were. Sherry?"

"Do you have vodka?"

Mackeson-Beadle uttered a gargling noise. " 'Fraid

16

not. Gin, of course. Tonic? Ice?"

"Thank you."

"Sit down, sit down. We must have a chat before Ronnie comes. Old chum, Ronnie. Comes every Wednesday for supper, and I go to his place on Sunday. You hit his night here. I don't like putting him off. We're both a bit set in our ways. Cheers!"

"Cheers!"

"Now, what's all this about marrying my daughter?"

AFTER THIS rather abrupt start we nevertheless discussed things in the English way, with the utmost politeness and delicacy, probing for clues to each other's intentions, shaping up during the first round while planning the eventual knockout blow, a kind of social rope-a-dope technique.

Old Mackeson-Beadle had a habit, which I welcomed, of falling abruptly into lethargy—as if into sleep though he was evidently awake—then springing back into lively action, only with no reference to what had gone before. The conversation was at times so random that it was like playing electronic tennis. As I remember, we talked a lot about marriage in general and about his own domestic bliss with Mousie before he was widowed. It was Mackeson-Beadle who set the pace, his voice first soft then booming, first low then bursting on my consciousness, like Haydn's Surprise Symphony. Yet I still couldn't keep my mind from wandering. While he was extolling his Mousie, for instance, the remark of that cynical doctor in one of de Maupassant's tales, describing marriage as an exchange of bad moods by day and of bad smells by night, lodged in my mind and stayed there like a tune on the brain. I had to fight back the urge to blurt it out.

We escaped just in time to the subject of his art collection.

I was amazed—to his satisfaction and delight—that the Canalettos on the walls, both of them, were painted by the master himself.

"Never know which is worth more—damn burglar alarm or the pictures," he said with a chortle. "Wouldn't want 'em pinched though."

"No, they're beautiful."

Mackeson-Beadle nodded enthusiastically. It seemed he was neither poor nor philistine. For a moment, the prospect of having him for a father-in-law seemed a little less appalling. But when we got onto politics it was easier to remember that I am constitutionally averse to the very idea of in-laws.

"So you see, Gull," he declared, toward the end of a longish (and loud) monolog on island politics, "we have to watch out. They're always trying to hem us in, can't leave us alone. Conservatives're no better than those wretched socialists in power now. All of them over there at Westminster, they're as bad as each other. A strong *man* with the right views, that's what's needed. As Ronnie says, a man who won't bother us with all that equality nonsense. Y'see, we have a long tradition of independence here. The Queen, you know, we call her the Duke of Normandy. Oh yes, you can smile, young man, but that's what she is to us. Ancient charters and all that. Our statutes go right back to the Conqueror's time. I don't know how much you understand, being a foreigner . . ."

"Former foreigner."

"Quite so. But I mean you're *English,* not a Guernseyman. People over there think of us as a tax haven or else some kind of cheap holiday resort. Good heavens, our old Jarls chiefs, you know, those Jarls of ours were civilized while the English were still wearing woad. No, we have to protect ourselves, protect our history . . . and of course our standard of living."

"But with no estate duty on the Island, surely the rich don't find too much trouble—"

"Ah, there's Ronnie now!"

Just in time. I looked out through the window to the back garden hidden in the gloom of the damp evening. The moon was racing across the sky trailing tufts of black cloud, outlining a human figure.

Mackeson-Beadle stood up and flicked a switch by the mantelpiece. A brilliant light flooded the lawn, blotting out the moon but throwing into relief a stout, beetle-browed man whose features were immediately, sinkingly familiar. If I'd had the smallest suspicion that the dinner guest was to be Ronnie *Hisland,* now Sir Ronald Hisland, I would never have stayed. Any excuse to escape would have been fine. Now I was caught, condemned to dine not only with Mackeson-Beadle—who might still be tempted to reach for a horsewhip—but also with the uncle of a girl I'd been very fond of at one time, whose house had been the scene of a row leading to a categorical embargo placed on the niece in question. The fact that I was subsequently reunited with Diana Hisland (though still later we separated again) had by no means brought Sir Ronald and me into closer or more intimate contact.

The question was: Would he remember me? The argument had occurred some years ago, and he was of an age when memory fades . . .

He came through the French windows with the elaborate fuss of an English traveler reaching his hotel after a strenuous tramp through a deluge sent specially to try his patience. The business with umbrella, mackintosh, galoshes and "dreadful weather" gave me time to study him before he got a good sight of me.

Sir Ronald was little different from the Ronnie I had known. Stouter, but no less gruff; abrupt, cantankerous. He probably still thought of my former homeland, the Soviet Union, just as he did when he came back from his spell in Moscow as military attaché. I made a mental note not to mention Russia myself, and in particular not to rise to the bait when he brought up the subject. For as surely as the sun sets daily on Semipalatinsk, Sir Ronald Hisland would not be able to resist taunting me with stories of oriental cruelty, salt mines and bull-headed commissars.

"Now, Ronnie, I don't think you've met Vladimir Gull. Friend of my daughter's."

"Aha! Gull! Aha!"

The answer was yes, he did remember me.

"How are you, Sir Ronald?" I said, stretching out a hand in greeting. "Congratulations on the knighthood."

"So," he growled, ignoring my peace gestures. *"You're* the chap that's after Amanda, are you? Hope you've warned Godfrey. If not, I'd better do it myself."

"So you know young Gull here, eh, Ronnie? Well, well, excellent, excellent. What'll it be, the usual?"

Sir Ronald nodded. Mackeson-Beadle, treating with tact the allusion to my track record, shuffled off to his bar, a kind of adapted nineteenth-century trunk, lead-lined for tropical climes.

"Oh yes," said Sir Ronald, left alone with me. "I remember you. The sentimental Russian. Been there recently?"

"No, I'm sorry to say."

"Sorry?"

My reply was exactly the excuse he needed to get him going again. I'd fallen into his snare even before he'd got the first drink in his hand. But again I was saved just in time, for Mackeson-Beadle came back bearing a glass of South African medium-sweet sherry and diverted the conversation to a subject that was evidently the basis of a running battle between the two "old chums."

"Y'see, Ronnie," he announced without preamble. "You were wrong!"

"Not at all, not at all," Sir Ronald shot back, leaping into action unreflectingly and forgetting, it seemed, that I was even there, as if triggered into his obsession on a signal from a hypnotist. "Anthrax germs are more deadly than Plutonium-239 only, I assure you, *only* when in artificially high concentration. Checked it with a chemist chap. I've no idea where you got your information, Godfrey. Anyway, it's wrong. And plutonium's twenty thousand times more toxic than cobra venom or potassium what'youmacallit . . . cyanide. Not twice, as you suggested. No imagination, that's your trouble, old fellow. No imagination."

"Cheers!"

"Cheers!"

Mackeson-Beadle shot his adversary a who-cares-about-the-details look and turned to me, perhaps hoping for an expert opinion in his favor. If so, he was not in luck. Much as I would have liked to help refute Sir Ronald Hisland, my knowledge of the properties of plutonium—239, 238, enriched, reprocessed, or otherwise—was a hodgepodge gleaned from a few international conferences for which I had interpreted.

So I merely asked, "Why the interest in plutonium?"

"Ah!" said Mackeson-Beadle. "You don't know. Of

course, how could you? Ronnie here has got a bee in his bonnet. He thinks we're all in danger. Or could be."

"No doubt about it, Godfrey, we are. We—"

"Y'see," Mackeson-Beadle continued firmly, "there's this damn great factory that makes the stuff over on the other side of the water, on the French side, I mean. You probably saw the place, up on the cape there, it's—"

"I saw only clouds," I said, "but I know where it is."

"Ah, well, that's where they process the stuff. La Hague." He pronounced it like the whiskey. "Frogs are turning out this fearful stuff by the ton and Ronnie here thinks they don't take the proper precautions. For years we thought it was just a power station. No terrible harm in that. But it jolly well isn't. It's nothing but a bomb factory."

"Bloody great bomb itself," interjected Sir Ronald. "Could explode any minute." He waved his drink, spilling it.

"Of course if the stuff escapes and the wind's blowing in our direction, you can imagine the problems *that* would create."

"Problems!" Sir Ronald barked. "D'you know, Gull, all you need is what you can shove inside a golf ball to make the most God-Almighty explosion? If you breathe in ten millionths of a gram—just a speck of dust—you get lung cancer." He coughed, half drew out his pipe, put it back in his pocket and handed his glass over to Mackeson-Beadle for a refill. "I've had what you might call a military background. I understand these things. I know you can't let things drift. Godfrey just refuses to recognize how damnably dangerous that plutonium is."

"Of course I do," the other man replied from over by the "bar." "You've been telling me so every day for the

22

past month. You're getting obsessed, old man. Bee in your bonnet."

"But what you don't understand, man, is the danger *we're* in. Good God, I don't give a damn for those Frenchies over there. They put the stuff there in the first place, that's their own lookout. No, I've told you before and I'll tell you again, we've got to do something."

"You know there's nothing—"

"Something to show 'em they can't just carry on regardless on our back doorstep. This is England here, like it or not. That's the trouble with everyone nowadays. They go ahead and leave us out of the reckoning. We might as well be in the mid-Pacific for all they care in Paris. Or in London, come to that. Thanks. Excellent sherry."

"Just the usual."

The door opened timidly, and the maid's head slowly appeared in the gap. "Dinner is served, Mr. Mackeson-Beadle."

"Good show. Thank you, Chambers. Come along then, both of you. We'll carry on over something to eat."

"Something to eat" was obviously how Mackeson-Beadle saw a meal. Food was fodder; no nonsense about cuisine. We started straight into a piece of roast beef that I could swear had not been roasted at all but boiled to a dark-gray color with the texture and appearance of gutta-percha. Maybe Mackeson-Beadle was an old Malaya hand? This "beef" was served with black-eyed potatoes and cabbage like the dregs of week-old *shchi,* which even the Russian peasant would have discarded from his soup pot. As a second course, the trifle, pepped up by the dregs of the South African sherry bottles which Sir Ronald had not managed to consume, resembled a vat of miscellaneous raw materials before the machine is switched on to blend them into plastic. The Stilton, on the other hand—which followed the trifle and was eaten with digestive biscuits—was not at all bad, even if excessively preserved with dollops of port.

But the wines . . . the wines were first class. A '64 Vosne-Romanée with the "beef," followed by a '59 Montbazillac and a decanter of vintage port. There was a great deal of ritual, which displayed both snobbery and knowledge, at the first quaff of each of the wines.

Mackeson-Beadle was one of that curious but far from rare species of Englishman whose excellent taste on a few elevated matters such as art and wine is in stark contrast to a lack of everyday sensibility concerning their minor comforts and surroundings. The ocher-tiled fireplace and the Canalettos, the "beef" and the Vosne-Romanée . . . it was hard for me to imagine the same man apparently not noticing the one while so thoroughly appreciating the other. A very English contrast.

They were, I supposed, an anachronistic species, the two old men. Yet, with their money, surely not without power and influence. My Marxism-Leninism teacher in Russia, not knowing then such expressions as "knee-jerk reactionary," would have described them as "feudal relics, maintaining the bourgeoisie as the ruling class through the manipulation of capital and social prestige." When I left my communist homeland, I thought I'd never find such animals, that they *must* be figments of perfervid Soviet imaginations. But here they were, genuine, almost interchangeable, relics—or so I thought.

The conversation at table did not revert to nuclear dangers until the port had emerged as the stayer in the field and the maid had gathered the debris before retiring. We talked—at least for the most part they talked —of the things such men discuss after dinner. I recall schemes to repatriate the blacks, modern lack of initiative, the morals of youth in general (but not, thank God, of Amanda—or Diana—in particular), the inadequate penalties for terrorism, and the merits of their respective cabin cruisers.

Only when we adjourned to the drawingroom and settled in armchairs did Sir Ronald return to his primary obsession. Like Tweedledum and Tweedledee, these tubby old men loved nothing better than a battle. Plutonium, I could see, anticipating a prolonged conflict, made an excellent substitute for a brand-new rattle.

"It's my considered opinion," Sir Ronald said suddenly and with a dreamy, manic look in his eyes, red with drink, old age and violently held prejudices, "and I can tell you I've given it a great deal of thought, that it would be child's play to actually get hold of some of the stuff."

Mackeson-Beadle was subsiding fast into lethargy again. "So you say, Ronnie, so you say."

And so saying, Sir Ronald extracted from one jacket pocket a wizened briar and from the other a tin of tobacco. He thrust his pipe between his lips, wrinkled his nose, opened the tin with a flourish—it was a mixture prepared by Fox's of Sackville Street—and began stuffing.

"But what exactly do you mean by 'getting hold of the stuff?' " I found myself asking him, forgetting again, in the atmosphere of alcohol and pipe tobacco, that I'd vowed not to encourage the bastard.

"What do I mean? Godfrey here'll tell you. I mean

25

taking it. Just that. Then turning around and saying, 'Go away! Leave me in peace! Take that bloody great factory and put it in Paris if you like, but not on my doorstep. Not where you'll kill Guernseymen with it. And get on with it or I'll bloody well blow you up!' "

"And blow yourself up, and everyone around too."

"God, I'm old enough, Gull. Never mind about me." He sucked hugely and exhaled a cloud of perfumed smoke.

"It wasn't you I was worrying about," I replied. "What about all the other people on Guernsey? How would they feel if you sat here with your cellar full of plutonium making atom bombs and unpleasant threats? That'd be far more dangerous then what's going on at present over at La Hague, surely."

"They're all behind me here. They're as fed up as I am. We're a united island. Full of team spirit. What we tell anyone who comes over and starts a fuss, starts criticizing, is this: 'There's a boat in the morning. If you don't like us, there's a boat in the morning.' Goes for you too, Gull, if you—"

"Hmmm," said Mackeson-Beadle, realizing that his friend was beginning to run amok. "Looks like it's clearing up outside. Should be able to get in a walk tomorrow. Up toward Moulin Houet."

Ronnie glared uncompromisingly at the space between myself and his old chum.

"Those '*châteaux,*' the French call 'em, you know, those lorries that carry the spent nuclear fuel they've used up in the power stations and take it to the factory there for reprocessing, whatever you call it . . . sounds like cheese. Anyway, I could get hold of one of those as easy as pie."

"That's right," I said, trying to apply a touch of brake

to his runaway fantasies. *"Châteaux.* I remember that term from a conference I worked at once in Washington. The English call them 'flasks' or 'coffins'. Then a problem arises when you're interpreting. Because the Americans, of course, don't say 'coffins' but 'casks'. An interpreter's job—"

"Easy as pie," Sir Ronald said as if to himself.

"But that's just spent fuel, not weapons-grade plutonium," I said, realizing diversion was hopeless. "It wouldn't be much use to you."

Ronnie swung around and looked at me fixedly. "You seem to know more about this nuclear business, Gull, than you were letting on."

"Well," I said, "I've done the interpreting at a number of conferences where they talked about it, yes. But I know no more than the average person. It's a hot subject nowadays."

"Is it? Is it? Well, how many people know, then, that a few thousandths of a gram of small particles of plutonium, if it gets into your lungs, it can give you . . . what's it called, Godfrey? Fibrosis? Kills you in a few weeks. Did you know that, eh? How many average people know that?" Sir Ronald Hisland didn't pause for a reply but continued relentlessly, getting up to bang his pipe on the fireplace. "Y'know what they say? One chap working alone who'd got hold of about twenty pounds of plutonium what'youmacall it, oxide, and some regular TNT could build an atom bomb—a pretty crude one of course—just using equipment and materials you can buy at an ironmonger's and from the chaps who sell scientific stuff for laboratories. I tell you where I got all this from, a report put out by the Ford Foundation. The Ford Foundation, no less! Not some ridiculous left-wing pamphlet. I've been boning up since I first found

27

out what was going on over there."

And he waved a hand in the general direction of the French coast, standing now, warming his bottom in front of the dying log fire. "No, no. I'm telling you, I haven't been so angry since . . . since I had to deal with those Russians. Now look here, Godfrey, I don't care what you say about Common Market regulations and safety standards . . . You always were a bit soft. I mean look at you—now consorting with damn communists like Gull." He got to his feet and I thought he was going to attack either or both of us. Was he frothing at the mouth or just salivating excessively? "You think I don't —"

But Mackeson-Beadle, finally, had had enough.

"Stop that, Ronnie," he declared, holding up his hand. "We've been over it all before. Gull and I have some . . . personal things to discuss. It's getting damn late. We'll carry on another time. Sunday at your house?"

Sir Ronald fixed his friend with what I can only describe as a demented stare.

"Don't think I'm going to let the matter drop. Good God, no. You know me."

When Godfrey Mackeson-Beadle merely looked up at the ceiling, Sir Ronald, with a shake of the head as if returning to the real world, shoved his pipe back into his pocket, ignoring the sparks that flew out during its abrupt downward journey, and groped for his umbrella, his mackintosh and his galoshes. He finally unearthed them from where "that damn maid of yours" had put them—in the umbrella stand, on the coat rack and on the shoe rack, respectively.

Eventually he trooped back through the drawing-room and out into the garden through the French windows. He didn't wish either of us goodnight. Mackeson-Beadle shut the curtains and walked unsteadily to the mantelpiece to switch off the floodlight.

"Getting more eccentric every day, poor old boy," he said, pouring himself a whiskey. "Too much money, that's his trouble." He dropped his voice to a whisper. "Not a real Guernseyman. Lives in Fort George." Then he said, in his normal voice, "Care for a nightcap?"

"A small one."

"Say when. When? Really? Hmm. Now, what's all this about marrying my daughter?"

I WOKE next morning in my bedroom at the back of the house after a night of dry-mouthed, tremulous sleep mixed with dreams of holocausts, of Sir Ronald's niece Diana, and of Amanda, who gave birth to a monster. Through a gap in the curtains I could make out a gray sea, white-flecked with foam and streaky sunlight.

I lay back, hardly daring to get out into the unheated room, and took stock of last night's meeting with my prospective father-in-law.

It wasn't going to be easy. He'd known all along that she was pregnant, even though he had made me tell him. Perhaps he just wanted to see if I would be honest. A mark in my favor, then. But what I didn't say to him was that I had no intention of marrying his daughter. It would have been neither polite, nor, under the circumstances, relevant.

We hadn't reached any decisions, nor had he pressed me for one. As far as he was concerned, if Amanda had chosen this not-so-young foreigner with a British passport and more . . . experience than was good for him, that was her lookout. He was, in many ways, a man of the world himself. Besides, Amanda had been married before, she was no innocent virgin; and I earned enough as an interpreter. Instead what happened was that talk of her "bun in the oven" set Mackeson-Beadle off onto indiscreet reminiscences of his own youth, stories which he had kept to himself before his wife died but which he now seemed relieved to share. The evening ended in this vein, with the whiskey slowly seeping into his memory, his words becoming less and less coherent, more and more frequently interrupted by yawns. At last I got up just as he was about to fall asleep in his chair, thanked him for the excellent wine and took myself off.

Now, within hours, I'd be back with Amanda. Mission accomplished, I supposed. I was fond of the girl, very fond really. I just didn't see her as a wife . . . or anyone else as a wife for that matter. Perhaps a child, that I might like, or was that mere vanity? A girl or a boy, no matter, but she preferred to have a child whose daddy lived in. I didn't blame her, although it was on this point that the argument always got stuck.

This subject was one of several about which she found it hard to control her considerable temper. Another was leaving the wash to dry. I told her this was a ridiculous thing to get angry over—especially *my* laundry in *my* apartment. But it was a blind spot of hers. She didn't mind my drinking; she probably more than matched me. She wasn't particularly concerned whether or not I kept strictly faithful to her, although I was expected early in our relationship to be on call. Yet suddenly she would start screaming at me because there were blotches on my knives or a rim around my bathtub.

It was during those scenes that I realized what a gnarled old bachelor I was becoming.

My Amanda. Oh no!

The telephone rang twice below, then someone picked it up. I decided I should risk getting out of bed and go in search of coffee when I heard Mackeson-Beadle's voice.

"Gull! You up, old boy?" He shouted up the stairs. "Like to talk to you, if you're ready."

Talk to me? Hadn't we said it all last night?

I suppressed a groan and instead made agreeing noises. Then I leaped out of bed and into yesterday's clothes, already draped over the back of a chair. Shaving could wait.

I found Mackeson-Beadle still in his dressing gown, as unshaven as I, looking worried.

"Most extraordinary thing," he began without preliminaries. "Maybe you can advise me, Gull. You seem a level-headed sort of chap."

"What's happened?"

"It's Ronnie. Just rung up. Sounded quite out of his mind. I thought that last night he was tipping the balance a bit. He started off again about my not taking him seriously, you know. So I told him, I think you're getting a bit out of kilter, it's not as bad as all that. Well, he went quite mad. Started screaming and shouting. Then he made a bet with me. Of course, I had to take him on. Doesn't do to refuse a chap like him. Takes it very seriously. And with him in such a violent—"

"Bet?"

"He bet me a thousand quid he could steal some nuclear stuff from the French thing over there. Inside two days."

"What?" I said, alarmed. "He's what? Going to steal nuclear material? Come on. I know what he said last night, but he's joking, bluffing."

"I doubt it. I really do."

"Then he's mad. You mean you actually took him on?"

"What else could I do?" moaned Mackeson-Beadle. "He can't possibly do it. And I could use the extra thousand. It wouldn't make a hole in his pocket, but life's getting more and more expensive for those of us who live on pensions . . . Besides, he said he'd go ahead and do it whether I bet him or not. He sounded . . . well, I haven't heard him quite like that before."

"But how does he possibly think he can steal nuclear material, just like that?"

"Oh, you don't know Ronnie. Well, you heard him carry on. Look here, get on and help yourself. I think Chambers has got some tea on the boil. I . . . I don't think I should talk to anybody else on the island about this. Ronnie made me swear to keep this just between ourselves. I think he regretted telling *me,* once it was out of the bag. But I suppose if you're going to join the family, I'd best start treating you as my son-in-law straight away. Eh?"

I reached across the white plastic-filigree breakfast table to a pot that Chambers had just deposited there while Godfrey Mackeson-Beadle was talking. It turned out to be coffee, of sorts.

"Oh yes, sorry. Help yourself. There's toast and marmalade. I told Chambers to make a good lot. I'm sure this will all blow over. But I do wish Ronnie wouldn't get these bees in his bonnet."

"Oh, has he put on this act before?"

"I wish it were an act. No, anyone else and I'd be less worried. Y'see . . ." and he looked at me with a deflated, hangdog expression, ". . . Ronnie got very taken up with those . . . private army things. Remember when there were a whole lot of strikes and things over there in

England, the utility workers walked out and all kinds of people, and chaps like us said, well, really, this won't do, we'll have to run the show ourselves? Some people took that pretty seriously, started building up their own organizations, pooling money and so on. Most of it came to nothing, of course. A lot of old colonels making silly orders of the day and I don't know what. They got pretty badly exposed in the press and so on. But Ronnie's sort of a big chief here on the island."

"How do you mean?" I asked.

"Well, socially. We're rather fond of social clubs, committees, that kind of thing, on Guernsey. Ronnie most of all. It's a kind of defense, I suppose, against the English invaders. You'll forgive me, but that's the way we Guernsey people see it. Of course Ronnie being English really, he's more Guernsey-proud than the real Guernseymen, but that's the way it often is. Then of course the really new chaps get themselves together into more and more clubs, just to show they belong, you know, and so it goes on. The private army thing, I must admit, that's going a bit far, not quite your regular sort of club. But then he's pretty rolling, you know. Can indulge himself. Lives in Fort George, and all that." Mackeson-Beadle gave a deprecatory cough. "Not from the Diplomatic, of course. He came into a lot of money from aunts and one way and another."

"Just a minute," I said, spreading a slice of toast with Cooper's Oxford marmalade as an antidote to the "coffee." "Are you implying that his private army still exists?"

"Not implying, Gull. Telling you. Of course, it's not very big, I don't think . . . probably just a handful of people really."

"Do they have weapons?"

33

"No idea. Not a clue. Ronnie told me before about the army thing of course. But he never trusted me to join. I mean I suppose I am his closest friend on the island. But he can't stand criticism, and I tell Ronnie what I think. Though he never takes the blindest bit of notice. I'm not quite so . . . well, not so Blimpish, you might say, as Ronnie. Though one does get into the habit round here . . . all this fief and seigneur business, bailiwick, that kind of thing. . . ." His voice trailed off.

"What about the local police," I put in. "Do they have any idea about this?"

"The Island Police Force?" He laughed. "Good heavens, they'd never even believe anything like that. They have enough problems already with tourists and stopping the kids throwing stones at the greenhouses. Nasty epidemic of that the other month. Besides, everyone knows Ronnie. He's been here on and off for years. His family had a house here. He's not one of the nouveaux, y'see, one of those who bought their way in. He wasn't born and bred here exactly . . . but he can do more or less what he likes. As I say, here on Guernsey it's still a bit . . . what you Russian chaps might call 'feudal.' "

I applied another thick coat of marmalade to a slice of toast and thought again, quite fondly, of my Marxism-Leninism teacher. He would have relished this situation. Certainly I was at a loss to know what advice to give. I wish I knew more about Sir Ronald Hisland and his island. How did Victor Hugo keep sane over here for fifteen years—twenty if you count his earlier stay on Jersey? Or weren't there so many prickly, exclusive Channel Islanders then, so many rich importees from England with their exaggerated nativeness? The real native islanders may have a long reputation of being proud, tightfisted and suspicious of foreigners, but they couldn't all have been Sir Ronald Hislands, surely. No French poet, not even the durable Hugo, could have survived very long if they had.

"Why don't you just ring him up and tell him you think it's a load of balls? He may have come off it by now."

"I doubt it. But I suppose I could try."

"You should try."

He sipped at a willow-pattern cup, making no move. I glanced at him and caught his eye.

"Oh, all right. Be back in a tick. Telephone's in the hall."

There was one all too visible in the breakfast room, but I could understand that Mackeson-Beadle didn't want to use it. I was alone for only a couple of minutes, time enough to recall my Marxism-Leninism teacher's other remark about the aristocracy in modern times: "An anachronism, but never underestimate an anachronism. The class enemy is never so dangerous as when it's isolated. Like a rat with its back to the wall and only moments to live." Was that Sir Ronald Hisland now?

When Mackeson-Beadle came back he was looking grimmer than ever.

"Told you so. All Ronnie said was, 'Not started yet? Better get a move on if you want to stop me. Paddle-steamer's fired up and I'm off to Cherbourg in ten minutes. Look slippy, old chap!' That's what he said, word for word. Then he laughed and hung up. You're right, Gull, he's mad as a hatter."

WE SAT silently for a good two minutes. Mackeson-Beadle seemed slumped in lethargy. Suddenly he shook himself—literally, like a dog that's just climbed out of water.

"By God, Ronnie may be out of his mind, but I'm damned if I'm going to let him get away with a thousand quid! Ten to one he's got hold of some stuff already and he's just going over there to pretend he's stolen it. Tricky old . . . Good heavens, does he think he runs this island? Does he think he can treat us real Guernseymen like . . . like clerks in the Foreign Office? Come on, Gull. You a good sailor? Well, too bad, too bad. Tell you what, call Amanda. Tell her we're taking the boat to Cherbourg. Tell her you'll go on from there. Come on, man. No skin off your nose! Get your things together. *Chambers!*"

I downed the dregs of my coffee. They were *both* mad, I decided. Two old English lunatics. And I was going to be son-in-law to one of them? Was I hell! Meanwhile, however, I might as well do the first part of the return journey by boat, since it couldn't be worse —or so I thought then—than the carnival ride operated by Aurigny Air Services.

But first I had to ring Amanda. The morning was starting badly. It didn't look as though it was going to improve. I shaved first, packed, then picked up the phone.

Amanda began true to form, answering the phone in her girl friend's house as if she knew it was me on the line.

"How'd it go?"

"How'd what . . . ?" I pulled myself together. "Oh fine, no problem. The conference was—"

"I don't mean the damn conference."

"I know. I was about to say that it went fine *and* your

dad and I get on like a house on fire. A towering in-
ferno."

"Ha-ha. How is daddy? Don't tell me. He's always as
right as rain. Not even you could faze him. When're you
coming back, darling?"

"Soon," I said. "But we're taking a quick side trip to
France first. We—"

"*What?* What're you saying, Vladimir love, for
Christ's sake? Or was it the line? Oh shit!" There was
a rattling on the line as she shook the receiver, emptying
it of the obstructive particles. "France?"

"Come on, love. France is on my way back. And
anyway it hasn't been a dirty word since the nineteen-
twenties."

"Is daddy there?" she snapped.

"Yes. Or not quite. He's getting the boat ready.
There's been a—"

"Oh, he's going too?"

"Yes, there's been a rather odd, well, there was a
friend of his . . . look, Amanda, it's not something I can
tell you over the phone."

"Like hell it isn't. When are you coming back to
England?"

"That's the problem. It's difficult to say exactly. I . . ."

"Okay, sweetheart, then I'm coming over."

How could I stop her? No way. Trying would only
succeed in raising a temper tantrum.

"Damn!" she went on in her practical voice. "I've
missed the ten-thirty plane. I'll take the six o'clock
tonight. The schedule's right here in front of me. I was
waiting to hear which flight you were going to be on
. . . or going to pretend to be on. It gets in at eighteen-
forty-five—*this* evening. Don't bother to come to Maupertus. We'll rendezvous down at the marina at seven-

37

thirty. I take it one of you will not be too busy to meet me there?"

"Amanda!" I said, unable to restrain myself. "You're crazy. I'll probably be back in England tonight. Tomorrow at the latest. Anyway, you weren't feeling too good when I left you."

She reacted with icy coolness—only it was like inverted Baked Alaska, with her hot temper trapped inside.

"Don't worry, darling, it's just the usual. That's what happens to women in my condition. It'll be good for me to have a break. Besides, I *love* Normandy. And it's so *close.*"

"For God's sake," I said, pleading into the wind, "it's the middle of bloody *December!*"

"Then we'll have it all to ourselves. Us and the natives. See you tonight, darling. At the marina. Seven-thirty. Be there!"

I sighed. "I'll be there."

"*Ciao,* darling."

She banged down the phone. I took a deep breath and went to pick up my suitcase. Outside the front gate a taxi honked. Mackeson-Beadle had sent it back for me, having gone on ahead to the harbor. He moved faster than I'd have thought possible. What did Guernsey *do* to people?

Chapter 3

December 14.   10:00 A.M.

HALF AN hour later we rounded the coast of Herm in the old man's thirty-foot cabin cruiser. The mid-morning sun played on the wavetops while a chill but light December breeze, coming from the west, bounced off the curved windows of the "bridge." The seventy-horsepower twin-screw Johnson engines sent a throb through the whole boat. I felt queasy.

"Of course," he said—twice—"I'd use the sail if we weren't in such a hurry."

"Of course," I agreed each time.

I knew the sunshine wasn't going to last because we were surrounded by low clouds, so low they hung down to the sea itself. The pool of light in which we sailed was diminishing all the time. The farther we went in a northeasterly direction, the more holes we had to punch through wisps and puffs of loose fog drifting to join the main fog bank off the French coast.

It must have felt something like this aboard the *Claymore,* that commandeered British corvette in which Victor Hugo, in his novel *Quatre-vingt-treize,* had his Prince de Lantenac cross from St. Helier, in Jersey, to France in order to lead the counterrevolution in 1793; and which came to a bad end in the fog, trapped between reefs and the Revolutionary fleet.

The *Claymore* had sailed at night, but that suddenly seemed an academic difference for we plunged now into a fog that made a mockery of clocktime, as if a time machine had dropped us back not just into night but into the Dark Ages.

"Good smuggling weather," said Mackeson-Beadle cheerfully. "Used to be like Hong Kong, y'know what I mean, the Islands. Regular trade of contraband to the French mainland. Tobacco, whiskey, wool, china, all kinds of things. Lots of our ancestors made fortunes that way."

I wondered if they'd also paid for Mackeson-Beadle's cabin cruiser . . . and his Canalettos.

"Good trade for the wreckers too," he went on, with a knowing smile; then sang out, "Keep her steady now!" He enjoyed playing the sea captain.

"Shouldn't we reduce speed?" I said tentatively.

"Nothing else out here, old man. Mad dogs and Englishmen! Safe as the midday sun. And dogs can't swim this far!"

So we sped on through the mist like some runaway Cleopatra's barge. At the same time the wind started gusting. The boat began to lurch more heavily, cutting into the waves that clapped together spurting foam off their tops. The big cabin cruiser splashed around like a toy boat in a bubble bath. Mackeson-Beadle held on more tightly to the wheel, humming a sea shanty. Beside him, I clutched a brass rail. I started thinking more fondly of Aurigny Air Services.

"On the edge of the race now, old man!"

His cheerfulness seemed forced to me, but I'm no sailor. I can no more handle boats than Red army tanks, or guns, or demanding women.

When Mackeson-Beadle had first told me that our route lay through the fastest sea current in the world, the Raz Blanchart between Alderney and the Cotentin, my first reaction had been, isn't there any other way? But he was a hundred percent confident . . . back at Greenacres. He'd done it a thousand times before, he said.

Only minutes after hitting the fog bank, however, I saw what I first thought was the shadow of our own cabin cruiser in the fog. My imagination was all ready to run riot, so I quelled my fear.

Seconds later I heard a scream. The thin remnant of a scream. I took it for a seagull's mew. I convinced myself. It wasn't easy. Mackeson-Beadle heard and saw nothing, though I pulled his sleeve and pointed out ahead at the fog.

Another scream penetrated the misty barrier. Human. No doubt this time.

"Slow down!" I yelled.

I made a grab for the sort of joystick that controlled our speed but stumbled and fell against the wheel.

"What the devil? Are you mad?" he screamed at me.

Only then did he too see the danger.

"Ahoy!"

Like a golfer shouting "fore!" when he'd just hit a drive at the heads of people standing in the middle of the fairway! Only we were the gigantic golf ball—and ahead was a diminutive, defenseless, suddenly and clearly visible yacht.

Nothing would have helped.

In the final seconds I saw a girl on board the yacht. Her screams were slicing through the fog's acoustic padding like a surgeon's knife. She was waving her arms. Her long dark hair, flying in the wind, half hid a heavily made-up face. The fog was no longer a barrier, we were bearing down so fast. Then she ducked out of sight.

Mackeson-Beadle hauled the wheel over. We yawed, slowed. But too late.

Our bow hit the stern of the yacht like a dodgem banging a slower car from behind; except our front end was sharp and there were no bumpers here. Splintering fiberglass and metal cracked and shrieked. Mackeson-Beadle, hurled against the plastic window of his bridge, cut his nose but hung on to the wheel. Because I had a split second to turn my back I got the impact on my shoulders. At the same time, I grabbed the lever, moved it by mistake back to full speed ahead, then yanked it into neutral. The cabin cruiser swung in an arc, then gave another solid bump to the yacht, side to side.

We were okay.

A tanker, compared to the miserable dinghy we'd hit.

I got my balance and ran out on deck to see how they'd survived.

Not too well.

The girl was screaming now for real. And for rage. The yacht, white with a blue slash around the hull—

interrupted now where a hole had been gouged to the left of the rudder—was keeling over. The waves slapped at it like hysterical women.

But what I hadn't realized was that there were several people aboard, packed in like illegal immigrants. One, with long gray hair tufting out from a yachting cap turned back to front, clambered out on the sloping deck, cursing volubly in French and making obscene gestures. Another, with a stolid weatherbeaten face, was tying his life jacket tighter while trying to shut off their outboard motor and get control of the tiller. He cursed in English. Another man, small and balding, shook the girl to stop her screaming. Yet another person was struggling into something orange and floatable inside the tiny cabin.

Out on the deck of the cabin cruiser I realized for the first time just how cold the seaspray was. And that the yacht was sinking.

Thank God one out of the seven of us had some idea of correct procedure in the matter of rescue at sea. The Englishman on the yacht, despite the angle of the deck, picked up one end of a coiled rope and tossed it across to me, so accurately that I caught it. With some heavy tugging and some help from the waves, I hauled the yacht up close to the cabin cruiser. At once a tall young man, in a tweed jacket under his orange life jacket and clutching a big black box, leaped over the gap and joined me.

"Don Gaffney," he said.

His accent was Brooklyn Irish, his face young but craggy. He wore glasses with thick tortoise-shell rims.

"Vladimir Gull," I said, tying a piece of the lifeline to the deck rail and hurling the other end to the man with gray hair, who broke off his cursing, fumbled, caught the rope and began tying an elaborate knot.

43

"Lash it quick and throw it over," I shouted in French.

The young American was busy behind me. "Okay," he suddenly yelled. "Hold it right there! I'm shooting."

Shooting?

Pirates? My heart skipped a beat.

But I saw what they were about. A film crew. The director with the long gray hair, the American cameraman, the English jack-of-all-trades, the decorative script girl in hysterics. Just one I couldn't account for, who didn't seem part of this archetypal film crew: the small balding one with steel-rimmed glasses.

"Quick, quick!" Mackeson-Beadle shouted from his vantage point on the bridge. His voice snapped me back into action. I lashed my end of the rope as tight as I could.

A bigger than usual wave crashed against the side of the cabin cruiser which then hit the yacht, inflicting another jagged wound.

"Get the girl over," I shouted.

She was in no fit state to make it by herself. She tried. That was the trouble. Her foot caught on the yacht's rail, and she toppled right in. Down and out of sight. Like a baby bird taking a premature flying lesson. Thank God she fell not between the two boats—or she'd have been crushed to death instantly—but off the front of the yacht. She was wearing a life jacket. But in this freezing sea she hadn't a chance if we couldn't get her out right away.

It was the small man in glasses who did the heroics; tied a rope around himself, leaped in and grabbed her. We all pulled at the other end.

"Hold it!" shouted the cameraman as they came up over the side, clasped together.

44

"Piss off, Don," the Englishman said, tugging at the rope and scowling at his colleague. "Bastard'll have you standing on the bloody yacht when it goes under if he can," he went on to me. "Slow, slow. Zoom in steady. Thinks he's a bloody Griffith."

The Englishman's face, naturally high-colored, was scarlet. He shook his head, covered with a tousled mat of yellowish hair like a field of ripe corn after a hailstorm, and gave another pull to the rope. The girl flopped on the deck, eyes and mouth gaping, like a played-out cod.

"Merde!" she gasped . . . and collapsed.

My stupefaction took a second or two to wear off. Then I hustled the girl down to the cabin. I began to undress and redress her from the store of blankets and old sweaters. Meanwhile up above the slanging match began. Hardly an even match. Mackeson-Beadle, knowing he'd been in the wrong motoring at breakneck speed through thick fog, could do little more than splutter apologies. His main opponent was the man with flying gray hair. The cameraman acted as chorus. The gallant rescuer, without his glasses, disengaged himself straight away and came in to replace me as nursemaid in the cabin—though the look he gave her wasn't as disinterested as it might have been. I followed his eyes and saw that the girl, in turning, had thrown off the blankets and revealed a plump white bottom. I gave the buttocks a slap and smiled at the shivering man before covering them up. He smiled back wanly.

"Pierre Denis," he said, extending an ice-cold hand.

I introduced myself, then went back up on deck. The Englishman was busy untying the knots in the ropes that held the two boats more or less together.

He looked up and saw me. "More trouble than it's

bloody worth," he said with a cheerful wink. The ropes slid overboard. The film crew's battered yacht, once released, listed onto its right side and glided away into the fog, the tip of its mast dipping the water like the end of a fishing rod.

"What the hell. . . ."

The abruptly cut-off yell in French came from the bridge. I glanced up and saw the man with flowing gray hair watch incredulously as the yacht huddled lower into the water. Then he shrugged.

"Oh, *merde,* I don't give a damn." He turned and went back to the task of berating Mackeson-Beadle. But already it was a performance. There was no more to say. The old man wasn't trying to put up a fight. I think I heard him offer compensation, but his words were soft and blurred.

"Bloody hell," the Englishman beside me said softly. "I'm Bob Hardacre. From Yorkshire, in case the accent didn't give the name away. Ker-rist!"

"Vladimir Gull," I said, holding out my hand. We were about to shake when Don Gaffney planted himself between us, outraged at our lack of maritime manners.

"Y'know what," he shouted in my face, his eyes popping mistily behind his glasses. "That was the fucking-est stupidest thing I ever saw. What the hell'd you think you're doing? You don't know how lucky you are I got this thing off the wreck, man." He brandished his camera. "If that'd gone down I'd have dropped you in with it, you crazy bastard."

I paused a second. He was half a head shorter than me. Then I pointed at his camera. "You're right," I said equally. "It looks to me, and I'm a complete idiot about these things, a very fine instrument."

Gaffney glared, looked at his camera, cradled it in his

46

right arm. Suddenly he relaxed and gave the footage meter a playful chuck under its rim. "You're damn right," he said, already mollified. "It's a 35-millimeter Arriflex-2C."

I looked blank, then quickly adjusted my face and looked impressed.

"Present from his mum," the Englishman interposed. Bob, like me, was apparently given to peace and compromise.

"Only way she could get him out of her hair," he said. Gaffney smiled.

"And whose is the yacht?" I asked.

Bob winked. "Piece of junk. Pradal—he hired it. Gilbert Pradal's the director, the one who's making all the noise. *Still.* Hey, Gilbert!" Bob moved toward the bridge. "Shut up and let him drive us home again. Claire's down there and she—"

"Okay, okay." Pradal's head came around the side of the fiberglass partition that screened the bridge. He was beginning to enjoy his tirade, even though most of it ended up somewhere out in the fog and the parts in French were utterly lost on Mackeson-Beadle.

Bob took my arm. "I told the silly bugger," he said in his gentle, rolling Yorkshire accent. "Five of us on that crazy coracle. All in aid of pretty pictures of Channel Islands fog. Can you beat it? Asking for trouble."

He pulled out a pack of Players, the tipless kind with the bearded sailor's head on it, from somewhere deep inside his oilskins. He was the only one who'd thought to wear some.

"Here," he said. "I'm going down to the cabin. Less windy." He laughed. "And Don, for Christ's sake shut that idiot director up. You're the only one he ever listens to, though that's none too often." He turned to me.

47

"Come on, lad, you look bloody freezing."

It's true I wasn't dressed to resist for long this kind of seaside holiday. I had on just an old Burberry over a medium-weight cord suit and cashmere turtleneck, the latter a present from Amanda. It was pink.

Down in the cabin, Bob lit up and began to smoke quietly. The script girl, Claire Fouquet, had calmed down and was showing gratitude toward Pierre Denis, the young man with the thinning hair, by looking into his eyes more frequently than necessary.

When I came in I sensed both embarrassment and hostility directed toward me. I forestalled what I saw in Claire was going to be a show of outright hostility by an elaborate show of care for her condition, with appropriate apologies. It took a while but in the end it worked, and in time I was able to find out more precisely what they themselves had been doing out in the Raz Blanchart. They were making a documentary. The subject had a neat—if ironic—relevance to the cause of our precipitous journey. They were doing a propaganda movie designed to portray Cotentin as the world's "nuclear dustbin."

"What's your role in all this?" I asked Pierre Denis.

"Guide," he said. "Really I'm a schoolteacher. But I organize what anti-nuclear protests we can muster around here. This lot came along, so I told them they'd get a good picture panning across from the plutonium factory up on the Cap de la Hague to where they're going to put a nuclear power station, by the cliffs over there."

He sat up to point in the direction we were now going, due east. But of course the shore itself was invisible behind the fog-screen.

I put my head out of the cabin door and shouted up

48

to Mackeson-Beadle, "What's the new plan?"

"We land at Diélette," he yelled back. Now that he was under way again, the strength had come back to his lungs. "Nearest point on the French coast. Besides, it's where these chaps're staying. Tides are favorable. It's an hour and a half to high. Just right."

I pulled my head back in. "But there's something I don't get," I said to Pierre. "What the hell did you expect to *see* on a day like this? Long shots in dense fog aren't—"

"*Mais non,*" he replied. "It was beautifully clear for about three kilometers from the coast. We were not paying attention. We were filming when suddenly the fog enveloped us. Nearer to the shore, the weather was limpid. Scintillating. Really."

And at that moment, as if on cue from Cecil B. DeMille, the fog bank evaporated. The cabin cruiser pushed its big, white, only slightly scarred nose out into brilliant sunshine.

EVEN IN midwinter the Cotentin coastline was startlingly beautiful. The muted rock grays, grass-greens and dune-browns harmonized against a tall aquamarine sky—one of those luminous moments when the clouds in the crystal ball vanish and the future looks bright, even attainable.

Pierre brought me back to reality.

"The plutonium factory," he said, pointing with an ominous finger. "*That's* where they do their dirty work."

"Where? Where?"

Don Gaffney, his French evidently good enough to

follow our conversation, put a hand on my shoulder and peered past my head.

"You see the cliff that sticks out, the Nez de Jobourg?" Pierre said.

"Yeah. Joe's nose."

"Up to the right."

"That's not bad."

The cameraman ducked back, picked up his funereally black equipment and, muttering something about "ten feet unused on the spool," went out to do a quick embalming job on the panorama.

He pointed his lens high up to the cliffs on our left, where a serried mass of flat-topped concrete buildings made incongruous square shapes on the fluid lines of the moorland horizon. Positioned in the center, an enormous red-and-white-striped chimney stack pierced the pure-white boxes like a rocket thrusting up from its launching pad. The factory had the look, even at a distance, of some futuristic space colony, suspended on the soaring uplands which, in the shimmering light, distorted by patches of mist that clung to the wavetops below, could themselves be mistaken for clouds. I shuddered.

Pierre had seen it too many times before. He nodded his head calmly.

"Looks like they're making vacuum cleaners up there, doesn't it? All white and modern and clean. But that's just the tip of the iceberg. Underground they've got vast areas of space, enormous pools like swimming-baths to absorb the heat of the irradiated material when it arrives, labyrinths of laboratories, vats, pipes, storerooms, offices. Everyone wears protective spacesuits. The stuff is handled by remote control, but even so there are accidents. The pipes are always falling apart and someone has to go in and patch them up with sticky tape. The place looks like a nineteenth-century hospital kitchen inside, even though it's only a decade old." His words came out in a tumble, vigorous but not angry.

"And they're still building, I see," I said.

"You bet. Cranes either side and round the back. The only other place that reprocesses plutonium is Windscale, in England. At least over there they agonize a bit. Not so much as the Americans who've put a stop to the whole nonsense. But in France it's grab the profits and run, and to hell with public opinion. We get Japanese stuff here, oh, from everywhere."

"And what's security like?" I asked, as casually as I could.

"Security?" Pierre laughed. "There's a friend of mine in security up there as a matter of fact. But what can he do? He's—"

"A friend?"

"Certainly. Even though I organize the protests. But his job's essentially the same. I mean, to prevent the worst happening. We just go about it in different ways."

"Uh-huh."

Yes, Pierre Denis could turn out to be a useful source of information, I thought to myself. He'd know the whole nuclear scene locally . . . from the inside. For another thing he must know the local ultras, the kind of people Sir Ronald Hisland might contact if he were seeking assistance on the French side of the water. He'd know the vulnerable spots where Ronnie might be tempted to operate. Operate? Ronnie a terrorist? Every time I started to envision the details, my mind clouded over and the whole idea seemed ridiculous. I mean, I wasn't even sure—once I thought about it closely—what Mackeson-Beadle and I had come over to *do*. Find

Ronnie—okay. And if we couldn't, what then? Contact the police? Warn the security people at the plutonium factory? Well, that was more plausible. Oh, hell, it was Mackeson-Beadle's problem. It was his thousand quid.

The old man's only firm plan had been to contact a friend of his in the *capitainerie* at Cherbourg, the outfit that guides the boats into the harbor. Now he'd have to ring him from Diélette. That made no difference. The point was the guy in the *capitainerie* also knew Ronnie . . . and his boat. He'd be able to tell Mackeson-Beadle if Ronnie had tied up there.

On the other hand, *my* only firm plan was to meet Amanda. At . . . when was it? Christ, get it right! Six-forty-five? No, that was when the plane got in. Seven-thirty. That was it. At the marina.

Still a few hours of freedom.

I'm mad, I realized. Crazy. Easier to imagine Ronnie running amok with an H-bomb than me tied for life to Amanda. Yet here I was running around in circles with the tether already chafing my ankles.

I wasn't free at all. Not even, it seemed, when she was in England and I was in France.

I had no childish desire to live a life free from all entanglements. Such a life would be dull and empty and unbearably selfish. What gave me the feeling of suffocation was . . . Amanda.

What was it about her? Nothing obvious. If it had been I wouldn't have fallen into her trap. She wasn't even an undercover bitch. An undercover puritan, yes. But that was forgivable. Maybe I'm a bit of one too . . . although that trait takes some surfacing now, I admit. As a young man I was sterner.

I suppose it all comes down to her . . . possessiveness. A man in tow was a habit of hers. Her husband's slipping from the leash left her with an empty collar. That made her feel ridiculous. That much I could understand. But instead of throwing away the leash, she went on safari to find some other animal to lead around. After several misses, she hit on me. I guess I was napping under a bush or something.

However it happened, the fact was I was possessed— in both senses. Like that time, for instance, three weeks after we met, she cooked a four-course dinner . . . and *then* asked me to drop by. On a later occasion she arrived at my place in Kensington with six rolls of Laura Ashley wallpaper to "do up" the bathroom. It was in a bad state, sure, but all the same . . . .

Yet I'd taken her incursions equably enough, in fact I'd been amused at the unabashed way she led me around in circles. It was a novel experience for me. So novel I didn't see the danger. I remained, in my way, fond and flattered. And fooled. And now we were going to be a threesome. A triangle. The geometry of it all was disturbing.

I looked mournfully out of the porthole, but the visual message was cut off between eye and brain by a mix of memory and self-pity.

Would I have to defect *again*—back to Mother Russia?

Then—fortunately—I was distracted by a groan from the couch behind me, and Claire Fouquet turned in my direction. Bob had nodded off. Pierre reacted first, his attention switching from me to the girl as if activated by an electric signal.

"Warm enough, Claire?" he asked.

She nodded.

Claire—"la script"—had more color now, though she wasn't the type ever to develop a peasant bloom.

53

The long dark hair, tamed now by a comb forced into the high crown, revealed her round face in which a large mouth and big round green-brown eyes dominated a small nose. Traces of make-up gave her a kind of patchwork look.

"Never fucking again," she muttered, and turned back to the wall, pulling the blanket around her.

Pierre laughed softly, looking wistfully at what he knew was a naked bottom beneath the coarse wool.

"Dunking a Parisienne in the sea in December . . . that's movies for you," I said.

There was a short, awkward silence.

"You're from around here?" I asked Pierre—just to keep things sweet.

"I teach at Les Pieux. That's a town nearby. In the CES."

"CES?"

"Oh, I forget you're not French. Collège d'Enseignement Secondaire. I cram them with tidbits from our glorious past before they go out and plant potatoes."

"How did you get turned on to nuclear protesting?"

"When they decided to build a nuclear power station. Right there." He laughed hoarsely. "Where I live."

His finger pointed. Along the line of his arm I saw a white tower at the base of a granite promontory almost in a direct line ahead, but slightly to the right.

"You see. A kilometer the far side of Diélette. My house is over the hill. That was an iron mine once. Those pylons there, you can just make them out. That's how they took the ore out, in buckets slung from cables, from pylon to pylon till they reached the last one, the big one like a platform there. Then the ore'd be transferred to boats. It's all coming down to make way for the nuclear power station."

"When?"

"Oh, a year or two, maybe less."

Shading my eyes with my hand, I could just make out the line of four rusty towers, like offshore oil rigs on a tiny scale, linked by wire ropes and tottering at drunken angles on concrete pillars sunk into the seabed.

"That's the Flamanville cape," Pierre went on. "The power station's going to be just to the right of the old mine. Hell, when that was announced, that's when we all began to think of ourselves as living in a nuclear dustbin. The plutonium factory's bad enough. In fact, it's more dangerous than any power station, especially now it's ten years old and falling apart. But the two together, that was too much. So we started protesting. Not just me. The farmers came down in their tractors. All kinds of people. Threw everything into the sea. But the worst of it is, even before the place gets built, the whole atmosphere around here has changed. The old mine workers, you see, they've been out of work for fifteen years. So they said, sure, let's have the power station. They still think it'll give them work. So it may, in the very short run. Building roads, breaking up granite blocks, all the worst, toughest kinds of jobs. But it won't last. When—if—the terrible place is built, it'll just need a handful of technicians to run it, and the local people will be back where they were. Worse off, in fact. Because no one's going to build anything else, factory or whatever, anywhere near a huge nuclear installation like that. So the whole place is divided, bad blood everywhere. Plus of course the *flics*, the policemen. They're crawling all over, spying, bullying people who won't go along with the electricity company."

"You included."

Pierre smiled. "Oh, every day some new pinprick.

One day they'll arrest me for posting bills in the wrong place, something like that. You can get yourself pretty isolated in a place like this where people have been submissive for generations, for centuries. There's not much left of the William the Conqueror spirit." He laughed, again with only a grain of humor. "I'm careful not to give them a pretext. But the police've got the judges eating out of their hand. They'll find a way. Electro-fascism. That's the price of a nuclear state. That's . . . *Merde.* I'm sorry. It's my *bête noire.* I'll shut up. It isn't built yet. Not by any means."

"By gum, I'm hungry."

Bob Hardacre was awake and rubbing his stomach.

"You're in luck," I said. "Diélette's five minutes away. We're just outside the harbor."

"Better wake up Sleeping Beauty then."

He leaned over and planted a kiss on Claire's cheek. Without knowing who it was, Claire put an arm around his neck and pulled him down to her, uttering what sounded like a contented purr.

Pierre, beside me, tensed. His eyes glittered, fixed on the tender scene from which he was excluded.

THE TIDE had an hour to go before full when the cabin cruiser steered cautiously around the outer jetty of Diélette harbor, at the end of which a lighthouse thrust its tip into the air, showing red out to sea, green toward the land.

I joined Mackeson-Beadle and Monsieur Pradal on the bridge just as the color changed.

Diélette itself huddled before us, wintery and silent. The gray houses, mostly empty for the winter, their windows white-shuttered, glared back at us blindly.

56

There was nobody moving in the village. A damp chill clung to the granite walls and the granite cliffs and the sad vegetable gardens and the patches of gorse and scrub. Yet there was an almost tangible sense of resistance, an age-old indifference to the dark midwinter, a feeling of peace and inner solidity and confidence in the coming summer. Despite the chill, Diélette offered a curiously hospitable warmth.

Pradal, too, was studying the mood of the village as we drew steadily nearer. An intense expression exaggerated the deep lines on the movie director's forehead. There was a top-heavy look about him, with all the weight of his flowing gray hair and high crinkled brow balanced precariously on thin cheekbones and a long thin nose above an even narrower tapering chin. Every bit the continental aesthete beside the yeoman tweediness of Mackeson-Beadle, standing proud again on the bridge.

"I'll berth her just inside the little jetty," the old man announced, rubbing his nose where he'd hurt it in the accident. "She'll be all right there for a couple of hours at least. Three most likely."

"I 'ope the proprietor of my yacht, 'e will be there," said the director sharply, continuing to stare ahead. His accent when he spoke English was pure Maurice Chevalier.

"Invite him to lunch," I said. "He'll feel better about it with a glass of Calvados inside him."

Pradal smiled and looked across at me. "For lunch? No, I think I will face 'im later."

I nodded.

But it was going to be a nuisance. I'd no chance to talk to Mackeson-Beadle alone, but he didn't need me to tell him the matter of the rammed yacht was not

57

going to help us find Ronnie. There'd be endless form-filling and interviews. Except . . . maybe their "guide," Pierre Denis, knew somebody or something which might provide us with a short cut? With regard to the yacht . . . and Ronnie. I debated about telling him the point of our visit to France. But the "need to know" principle encouraged me to be silent for the time being. As for me, the phrase had a different meaning. I still needed to know, myself, just about everything.

"Safe in port! Lunch on me!" Mackeson-Beadle called out. "Owe it to you all."

Pradal broke out into a smile for the first time. Heads popped out of the cabin. Recovery was now almost complete.

"Yes, lunch," Pradal mused aloud. "I 'ope the *patron,* 'e 'as not forgotten us."

Inside the inner wall of the harbor the sea was calm as a mountain lake. Mackeson-Beadle showed no hesitation slipping in neatly beside the steps that angled back from the top of the jetty down to the sandy bottom. The last few steps were covered by the rising tide.

"Grab a line, Gull, there's a good fellow, and tie us up."

I jumped across the breach and wound a rope through one of the massive green-painted iron rings set into the granite blocks. The motor reversed, and the cabin cruiser came to a stop just where it should. The old man was demonstrating his best seamanship to offset his recklessness out in the fog. Bob Hardacre slipped another rope through the second ring and pulled the stern against the side of the jetty.

Across the water, the granite and glass façade of the Auberge du Vieux Port sent out flickers of light from its windows. The film crew didn't hang around, not with the nearby prospect of warmth and a free meal and booze. In less than a minute, Mackeson-Beadle and I were the only ones on the jetty, securing the big cabin cruiser, allowing slack for the variation of the tide and hoisting the yellow flag to tell any customs man who might be around that he was welcome to inspect the boat.

As soon as the mechanical tasks were done, Mackeson-Beadle began to show reaction to the hectic events during the crossing. His legs shook ominously. He tried to walk but had to clutch onto a stack of crab pots, which began to topple despite the dollops of concrete inside them. I ran forward and slapped the wicker baskets back into place.

"Thanks, old boy." Half recovering, he took the strain off his legs by sitting on a granite bollard strategically placed on the jetty. He put his head in his hands. "What a cock-up, Vladimir. What a frightful cock-up." Just as he had suddenly charged himself up into action, and almost literally flung us both across the water in one spontaneous burst, so now he'd completely drained himself of energy.

I put a hand on his shoulder. "Could be worse," I said. "You ran into a guy with a lot of nuclear information. Pierre Denis. He also has a friend in security up at the plant. We might contact the man."

"Suddenly it seems crazy," the old man said, as if he could see no point in following up any practical suggestion. "Unmitigated madness. Somehow Ronnie seemed real over there . . . ." He waved his hand in a westerly direction. "But now, seeing that big factory up on the . . . ."

But he couldn't see it.

The fog bank had drifted on shore, amalgamating all

the wisps of cloud into a solid phalanx that was marching unopposed over the massive cliffs on the Cap de la Hague. It was a matter of ten minutes before Diélette itself would be engulfed.

Mackeson-Beadle used my arm to lever himself up onto his feet. He was stiff and cold and still in a mild state of shock. He rubbed his bruised nose again.

Suddenly he shivered convulsively, then stood stock-still. I thought for a moment it was his heart. But he was staring fixedly down into the harbor. He raised an arm to point at the cluster of five or six small boats which the tide was just easing off the sandy floor, from which long ropes extended, fore and aft, attached above the high-tide line to anchors dug deep into the beach or to granite bollards on the sea wall.

"Ronnie!" he croaked.

"*What?*"

"I mean his boat. Look."

Huddled among the dinghies and rowing boats below us was one that looked newer than the rest, a little yellow runabout with its outboard motor tipped back and the name *St. George* painted in blue letters on the bow.

"*St. George.* That's Ronnie's boat. The little one he keeps slung on the back of his cruiser. It must be the same, same yellow color and everything. What's it doing here?"

"He's beaten us to it."

"But he can't have, he couldn't have . . . Not this little . . . ."

"Well, let's ask him."

"Who? What're you saying, Gull? He's not here, is he?"

I smiled.

"Sir Ronald? No, no. But there's a young man with flaming red hair down on the beach. If you follow along the rope from the yellow dinghy, you'll see the other end's attached to an anchor which our friend is right now digging into the sand."

Mackeson-Beadle came to life as if an electric charge had been applied to his plump backside. He pulled me along the jetty.

"I say! You!"

The man with red hair gave a kick at the anchor, then glanced up at us. He was dressed in a French fisherman's blue smock and heavy blue wool trousers. His expression was a mix of caution and fear. He said nothing.

"Whose is that boat? Eh?"

The man still didn't answer, but scowled at Mackeson-Beadle.

"You work for Sir Ronald Hisland?" I said.

"What's that to do with you?" His voice was low, but with an unmistakable Guernsey twang.

"Where is he, man?" Mackeson-Beadle had difficulty in keeping his temper and his voice down.

The man looked into each of our faces in turn and didn't seem to like what he saw. "Bugger off!" he said. Then he turned and walked quickly away up the sand toward the narrow road that separated the harbor from the terrace of the Auberge du Vieux Port.

"Hey!"

At the old man's shout the redhead took off. He ran straight up to the low granite wall that kept passing cars from tumbling into the harbor, vaulted over and was fifty yards away by the time we'd run as far as the road.

"What the hell," I said. "We'd never have got anything out of him. He wasn't the talkative type."

61

"All the same," Mackeson-Beadle said gloomily, "it's odd he's here already. Bad sign. Bad sign indeed, Gull."

THAT VERY moment the fog hit us. Sooner than I'd expected. One moment there was sunshine, the next it was all I could do to see the front of the *auberge* ten yards away. As for Mackeson-Beadle's cabin cruiser at the far end of the jetty, it was already out of sight. Very faintly a shred of green flickered out to sea as the lighthouse pulsed its green glow; it disappeared, came back, then blotted out altogether. A foghorn blared from up the coast.

"Come on. Let's get in the warm."

Mackeson-Beadle was keen to follow my advice. On our way across to the inn, he remembered he had to telephone the Cherbourg *capitainerie*. At the prospect of action, or at least information, he brightened.

"See you in a tick," he said, with a quick wave.

He left me in the diningroom.

Here the entire crew was already assembled around a big table, talking in loud voices and warming themselves with whiskey, *porto* and the flames from an enormous fire roaring in a granite fireplace raised about two feet off the floor. Closer to the flames, spitting and sizzling, was a *carré d'agneau,* a whole side of lamb. Tending it stood the *patron,* with the figure of a Rabelaisian monk and a beatific smile on his round face. He had certainly not forgotten that the film crew were expected back for lunch. As I approached, he took a thin butcher's knife and sliced off an outside chop.

"*Hein?*" he announced challengingly to the company. "Keep calm. Be patient. When it's ready, it's ready." He turned ponderously, like a heavy top on its

62

last revolution, and pointed a fat finger at me. "So this is the wrecker!" His bellowed laugh echoed around the large diningroom. "You nearly killed my only clients, *hein?*"

Grinning, he pulled the chop across his teeth like a mouth organ. A rivulet of hot grease ran down his chin, and he wiped it off with the corner of his already succulent apron.

Gilbert Pradal took the hint. Ignoring the absence of Mackeson-Beadle, he declared loudly, *"Allez!* We're all here. The oysters right now! In ten minutes we'll eat the lamb."

Pradal also appeared to have forgotten, or deliberately to have put off and out of his mind, the delicate business of contacting the owner of the sunken yacht. I wasn't going to remind him.

The *patron* beamed at his guests.

We were the only customers. December was very out of season on the Cotentin.

"Bon! Françoise! *Les huîtres!"*

The kitchen door swung open, and a buxom, black-haired, sweetly sweating girl emerged, bearing a platter of oysters which, despite muscular arms, she could barely support.

Corks popped in three bottles of Muscadet. The plates with motifs of fat-clawed crabs began to fill up with razor-sharp shells exposing their soft insides. We were ready to erase the discomforts of life at sea.

I sat down between the empty chair for Mackeson-Beadle and the script girl, Claire Fouquet. Pierre Denis was on her far side, and the three others sat opposite.

"Oysters," said Pradal, in a director's voice, "what exquisitely pertinent symbols of the Cotentin!" He held one up, so that we were all more or less compelled to

63

turn our eyes in his direction. His gray hair puffed out behind him like smoke as he looked at each of us in turn. "Prickly, secretive, salt-smelling, creatures of winter storms."

Mackeson-Beadle came in at this point, pulled out the chair beside me and sat down heavily. "Got through," he said in a loud whisper, "but no sign. I'll try again soon."

"He'd have done it in record time if he were there already," I said. "Give it twenty minutes. Eat, enjoy yourself."

Mackeson-Beadle looked at me wanly, then drained his glass of Muscadet in a gulp.

"Mustn't tell Amanda about Ronnie, for heaven's sake," he said hoarsely. His face was purplish red.

I nodded, but I was concentrating on the oysters. Mention of Amanda no less than Ronnie was a thoroughly unwelcome intrusion into what promised to be a great lunch—all the better for coming so soon after Mackeson-Beadle's domestic fare.

"Cosy as the cliffs of Greenland, *mes amis,* that is the Cotentin in winer. The last wild coastline of France." Pradal looked at his audience again to make sure they were paying attention. "Impossible to imagine June days, apple orchards, soft sleepy cows, scarlet sunsets at midnight."

"Can't say as I like oysters," said Bob Hardacre, swallowing one. "Myself."

"So much about this country is uncomfortable, is it not?" Pradal continued undeterred. "A spiny shell, a challenge, daring you to explore the secrets inside and pick out the pulpy flesh. Crabs, lobsters, sea snails, artichokes, all these prickly, secret things . . . and of course this delicious . . . oyster."

64

Pradal darted a look at Bob, aesthete to philistine, laid his head back, and with the gesture of a concert pianist held the oyster over his open mouth, bending his thin wrist before dropping it in.

"What about the mine?" Don Gaffney, the camera-man, said across the table to Pierre Denis, ignoring his director's effusions. There's always that same division in film crews, the trendies and the technicians. The cam-eraman adjusted the glasses on his bony Irish-American nose. "Could we get some shots when the fog clears? I could pan across from the site of the power station . . . old and new, get the idea? Looks like a weird old place."

"It is," Pierre agreed. He answered in French to Gaffney's American, but both understood each other. "Sinister. It was first started over a hundred years ago, that iron mine. It went bankrupt and started up again God knows how many times. It is certainly worth filming if you can. I will take you there. If it's really clear, you can see across to Guernsey. But even in the mist you would capture the derelict atmosphere. It's ghostly, if you believe in ghosts."

"I'd need a blue filter. Maybe . . . ."

"So, Vladimir. Tell me about yourself."

Claire's Parisian voice blotted out the rest of Don Gaffney's technical reflections like a radio announcer cutting across a routine discussion with a news flash. She was now looking like I imagined she wanted to look, repainted, wearing chocolate velvet jeans and a hugging sweater. I put on my seducer's smile, but auto-matically.

"Every man over forty is a scoundrel," I said, quoting Shaw.

I needed only one ear for the ensuing dialog, the scene

65

being all too familiar and overwritten.

With my other ear, I heard Don talking filters and lenses while Pradal ranted on to a bored but resigned Bob Hardacre, whose limited knowledge of French was no disadvantage.

"The spider-crab . . . weaving itself a web of seaweed, catching playful sprats in its slimy threads . . . imagine an image of the Fates, weaving their web of life under the sea, under the thudding waves of the Atlantic Ocean, suspended in impenetrable dark . . . ."

It sounded better in the original French. Flights of fancy always do.

Meanwhile Françoise returned and removed the oyster shells. The lamb was then brought on by the *patron* himself.

"*Voilà! Bon appétit!*"

He banged down a long dish of chops cut off the rack and sprinkled with rock salt which glinted on their crisp brown outsides and pink centers. Dishes of *flageolets* and boiled potatoes followed. Several bottles of a red "Réserve" were placed within easy reach. The *auberge* began to seem more and more like a haven—a heaven. The hellish shrouds of fog outside stopped at the windows, and inside all was warm, mellow, snug, continuing my first distant impression of the village. Bottles and brass candlesticks glinted on the mantel above the log fire. The smell of burning wood, charred lamb, wine, dark tobacco and the mingled scents of Claire and Françoise were sweeter than incense. I could willingly have stayed at this table for an eternity.

If only the *carré d'agneau* could multiply like the loaves and fishes; if only there were a magic porridge pot that could produce not oatmeal but an endless suc-

66

cession of *chefs-d'oeuvre* from the great tradition of French cooking. If only . . . .

More mundanely, Pierre began regaling Claire with his impressions of Guernsey. They weren't altogether favorable. I hoped not too much was getting through to Mackeson-Beadle, though there was no real danger. His French had hardly progressed beyond the *"plume de ma tante"* stage. Pierre managed to work up a high degree of wine-inspired indignation at the thirty merchant banks on the island, profits taxed at twenty percent, the iniquitous absence of death duties or value-added tax.

"Hell, if you've got money to buy your way in," he concluded, "it's a cinch. But, *mon Dieu,* I would not want to live there myself."

"Oh," said Claire, round-eyed, playing the innocent. "Why not?"

"Left-wing scruples. Utter nonsense," muttered Pradal, breaking off for a moment from his monolog and flapping his long hands in disgust.

Pierre ignored him. "Too many people, that's the real reason," he said, smiling at Claire. "I would miss the open spaces of the Cotentin. And then, of course, they'll be getting the nuclear muck from here, the radioactive effluents, the chlorine. That's the amusing thing. The currents will take it away from us here and deposit it all on English shores!"

He laughed.

"What I liked least about Guernsey," I said, "was what I heard in a pub over there. There must be something wrong about a place where they call a milking shed a 'mootel'. . . ."

"Un quoi?" said Claire.

67

"Mootel. What you might call a . . . '*mugitel.*'"

"*Quelle vacherie!*"

There was general laughter, except that Mackeson-Beadle was going glum under the influence of the Réserve du Vieux Port and his unavailing struggle to follow the French.

He pulled my sleeve. "Lost 'em before, you know." His words welled up from some earlier preoccupation.

"I don't follow," I said, turning toward him reluctantly.

"Amanda. She's lost 'em before."

"Lost what? Husbands?"

He must know I knew about husband Number One, a gallant but regrettably impotent major in the British army.

"No, babies."

I stared at him, I hoped not oddly.

"Never could get very far without some complication," he went on. "Not her fault, poor old thing. What's the matter?"

"Nothing. I was thinking that's too bad."

"Ronnie's not a man to be trifled with, you know. Just as well to take precautions. Thank God you came along, old boy. Very grateful." He looked at his watch. "I'll try again. Well, in a couple of minutes."

He drank another full glass.

"This army of his," he said, picking up his train of thought. I glanced across at Pierre, checking if he were paying attention to the old man. He wasn't, nor were any of the others. "Local thugs, far as I can make out. Not the sort of people I'd know socially. Ronnie's the only officer left, you might say. Used to make 'em do drilling, went on exercises about twice a month. It interfered with our dinners sometimes. Not recently. But he

68

would have told me if he'd packed it all in. Liked to have fishermen. Made communications easier, he told me once."

"You mean with the French mainland?"

"I suppose the fishermen came over. Don't know about Ronnie of course."

"But you'd never seen the man with red hair before?"

"Never seen any of 'em. Kept my distance. Had to."

"What about his politics?"

"Ronnie?" Mackeson-Beadle refilled his glass. "Well, you heard enough, didn't you? Living in Moscow, that life with foreigners, cooped up in little enclaves, well, you know about that, doesn't make you left-wing, does it? I remember a journalist chappie a few years ago. Went over to Moscow full of the joys of the Revolution. Came back a raving Bolshie-hater. Saw too much."

"I thought Sir Ronald was always a bit . . . on the right?"

"I expect so. He got into a bit of trouble in the thirties, if I remember rightly. Something about the Jews. But I thought he'd mellowed since then."

"Maybe not. On the contrary."

"Calvados! Calvados! *Patron,* we need Calvados all round with our coffee."

Gilbert Pradal's voice rang around the diningroom. The *patron*'s glistening head appeared in the kitchen doorway.

"*Tout de suite.*" And, as the door swung shut, "As if I wasn't going to put a bottle on the table anyway."

Coming back with the apple brandy, the *patron* decided that this was the moment to take it out on Pierre Denis. "Don't listen to his nuclear *merde*," he announced to the company in general. He folded his arms and stood at the head of the table. Even Gilbert Pradal

69

was overshadowed. "You see how dead the place is around here. Energy, that's what it needs. The energy of the future. You should have taken some pictures of the filthy old mine when it was working. Or the granite quarries when they were working. The whole place was covered in dust. Explosions all the time. Set that against shiny steel in a modern factory. Be fair, *hein?*"

Pierre couldn't resist arguing the point. So they, and eventually everyone with the exception of the preoccupied Mackeson-Beadle, got down to a prolonged battle, well fueled by Calvados, on the merits of nuclear energy. By the end Pierre was calling all pro-nuclear people ex-Nazi collaborators, and the *patron* was denouncing the protesters as Maoist wreckers and Pierre in particular as a biased, subversive, unrepresentative twister of innocent minds. Both were enjoying themselves.

Claire got some mileage out of teasing Pierre by taking the *patron*'s side. Yet Pierre, whose passions were genuine and profound, held his own against her easier, wittier cynicism.

"I'm a self-made man," Pierre protested. "Son of a local peasant. *You're* the outsiders, the *horsains*. You weren't even born here."

"You'll never persuade me," declared the *patron,* laughing. "Never."

Claire got up and kissed him on the cheek. Everyone cheered . . . and drank.

While Pierre set off yet again to attack the windmills constructed by the patron, Mackeson-Beadle glared once more at his watch.

"Yes, yes. I'll give him another try. He must be there by . . . ." His voice trailed off.

He got unsteadily to his feet and turned toward the

corridor at the back of the diningroom, which led to the *toilettes.*

"Hold the fort," he said, doubling back to grip my shoulder. "Hold the fort." Then, finally, he disappeared.

TEN MINUTES later, I reckoned I'd held the fort long enough and I went to see what the trouble was. Despite myself, I was impatient to have news of Ronnie Hisland. But the corridor was empty and the telephone wasn't telling if it had been used or not. I opened the door to the *toilettes.* No one was inside. I went back to the diningroom.

"Shut up a second," I yelled. "And tell me where the hell the old man went to."

No one had seen him.

I put my head through the kitchen door. The *patron* was fast asleep,, his big head cradled in his arms on the central table like a massive turnip among the remains of *flageolets,* potatoes and *carré d'agneau.* One elbow was tipping the enormous plate on which the lamb had been served; the sliding grease was congealing like candle-wax. But Françoise was awake, stacking dishes, and she told me she'd seen no sign of Mackeson-Beadle, that he hadn't been in the kitchen.

Curiouser and curiouser. I went out the back and around the side of the *auberge.* Still no trace. On a sudden impulse, I ran across the road toward the fog-shrouded jetty. Along the top my head was pounding, the Calvados swilling against those sensitive membranes on the inside of the skull. There was no sound apart from the muffled slap-slap of my shoes on the slimy granite. I reached the top of the steps that angled back down into the barely visible water below.

"Oh Jesus!"

The boat was gone. Mackeson-Beadle's, that is. The yellow dinghy was still where I'd last seen it. But the cabin cruiser was nowhere in sight.

I clambered down the steps to just above the waterline. A rope was attached to a small open rowboat of uncertain age and less certain seaworthiness, but serviceable. I unslid the rope and cast off. Using one oar, since that was all there was, I reached the dinghy in a series of zigzags, then stood up, wobbling, put my leg over the edge and half-tumbled in. Searching around, I found the usual things there are in small boats—a couple of life jackets, spare gasoline, paddle, coils of rope ... but also, inside the minute cabin, a radio set. To me, no professional, it seemed a very sophisticated kind of receiver-transmitter to have in a boat that size. If this was a sample of the type of equipment used by Sir Ronald Hisland's private army, it was very disquieting.

Finding nothing more of interest, I paddled back to the jetty.

Outside the *auberge* a voice rang out through the fog.

"Monsieur Gull!" The unmistakable raucous voice of the *patron*.

"J'arrive," I yelled back. I ran the last twenty yards. "Yes?"

"Eh voilà," said the *patron,* reverting to his normal growl. His eyes were red and he seemed not fully recovered from sleep. His right elbow shone with slimy lamb fat. "A message came through on the telephone. From Monsieur Mack . . . something or other."

"Yes? Mackeson-Beadle. What did he say?"

"It's off. The bet is off."

"What?"

"He spoke in French, your Mack . . . whatever. Terrible French. But I am sure that is what he said. The bet is off. Not to worry. All over. *Fini.* Bye-bye."

I RAN inside and grabbed Pierre. "Got a car?"

He nodded.

"Then let's go," I said.

He was as cool as he was quick. No bothering with explanations to the film crew. Besides, they were in a haze of *Calva* and wouldn't have listened even if Pierre had known what to say.

He unlocked both front doors of an old-gold Citroën CX 2000 with a gash on its front right fender and switched on the quartz headlights, sending a yellow beam into the *potage* of ground-level cloud.

"Okay. This is what it's about," I said . . . and told him everything. According to the "need to know" principle, I reckoned now was the time he needed to know everything I myself knew, which wasn't much. We got off to a slow start as Pierre wanted every detail accurately inscribed in his mind. But since progress through the fog was slow, we didn't lose anything by spelling out names, with some repetition of *"ka pour knock-out"* and *"el pour lamentable"* until he had grasped both barrels of Mackeson-Beadle.

I had thought to drive straight to the plutonium factory and contact security there. But Pierre modified the plan in view of the possibility—probability, he thought —that we were dealing with a nut rather than a genuine nuclear thief. Besides, they might not know how to take such a story coming from the leading anti-nuclear protester in the area . . . accompanied by a Soviet defector.

"C'est du cinéma!" he muttered. "One day it really

73

is going to happen. But not a *château.* Who needs the spent fuel? It is possible to make a kind of bomb from it . . . for example by destroying the cooling system, but that is too cumbersome. One day someone will steal the really deadly material, the plutonium oxide that they manufacture up there."

He nodded his head. We were winding cautiously up toward the Cap de la Hague. Not immediately to the factory, but, on his suggestion, to a café in the little town of Beaumont, a couple of kilometers this side of it. Pierre's security contact, Michel—a "mole" for the anti-nuclear movement as he described the man—always took a drink there about this time of day. We both agreed it would be best to go via a friend rather than confront the security service *en bloc.*

At Helleville crossroads, watched over by a morbid mold-green calvary, another car latched on behind us. For a moment I worried about being followed, then, as another and then another joined the line, I realized we were merely being used as a guide through the fog. It's always easier to follow red lights than be the first one through.

In the empty fogbound high street of Beaumont-Hague we abandoned the Citroën which, two paces away, dissolved into the murky old-gold light of the streetlamps. Picking our way through a huddle of Mobil gasoline pumps, we entered the front room of the Relais de la Hague. No one else was there. The benches were as depressingly vacant as the wooden forms of a Dickensian Ragged-School classroom during the vacation. The room was filled with a stale smell of cider, beer, red wine and Gauloises.

An old man with a humpback and the white stub of a Hitlerian mustache, the brim of a droopy felt hat almost covering his rheumy eyes, shuffled in from the back and peered at us.

"Has Michel been in yet?" Pierre asked.

"Ten more minutes," said the man.

"Do you have vodka?" I asked.

He shook his head scornfully. We both settled for a *coup de rouge*.

"So what's Sir Ronald Hisland going to do with his nuclear material when he gets it?" Pierre asked, having sipped the coarse wine and gingerly wiping his mouth with his sleeve.

I shrugged.

"What damage does he hope to cause?" he insisted. His glasses were steaming up and he took them off to wipe them. His blue eyes were bright and alert.

"Apart from a hole in Mackeson-Beadle's pocket, no idea."

"And his real motive?"

I shrugged again. "As my teachers used to tell me in Moscow, who knows of what the class enemy is capable?"

Pierre laughed softly. There was a long pause, during which we drank more wine as an alternative to thinking.

Eventually Pierre began again. "But you think, once he has proved his point—if he goes ahead with the idea, if it's not all bluff—then he will just . . . ."

"Then that will be it, I should guess. If he's got other ambitions, he hasn't told me. Or told Mackeson-Beadle, I imagine. Though it's odd both men disappearing like that, *and* their boats. Maybe Mackeson-Beadle did get through to Ronnie on the telephone after all. Maybe he wasn't spirited away unwillingly in his bloody cabin cruiser. They can't be in this together, I suppose . . . ? Hell, no." I paused, looking at Pierre's anxious face.

"Anything's possible, that's the trouble. Where the hell's Michel?"

My head, I realized, was unsteady, and my wine glass empty for the third time. Outside the café window the fog was beginning to swirl erratically in a rising wind. It was only half past four, but the street lamps stood in a kind of false twilight, as if technicians from a movie set had botched the lighting and got the timing wrong on their fog machine.

The wind intermittently seized some loose piece of plastic caught in a shutter, rattling it into a frenzy like a revving two-stroke motor, grating on my nerves.

The café was no haven from hostile elements as the *auberge* had been back in Diélette.

It seemed somehow a good idea to take a quick breather, even if that meant taking a virtual bath in the cold clouds at the same time. Pierre opted to nurse his head inside, in the warm.

Emerging into the shivering, damp evening air on the Hague moorlands, I was reminded of Russia. It is true what they say about Russians. They—we—do get drunk frequently. Is it the cold, communism, comradeship, or, as we say, the *russkaya dusha,* the Russian soul? Whatever the reason, a stomach topped up by coarse red wine and a head reeling from the combination of alcoholic fumes and ice-cold air quickly made me forget the patina of western, British, "civilization" with which I disguise myself. I felt at one with my ancestors, generations of Russian peasants. We have a proverb, "If you drink you die, if you don't drink you die, so you might as well drink."

Yes, well.

Outside, marching along the pavement, alone in fog-bound Beaumont, as desolate as Siberia at that moment,

I recited loudly, in Russian, a line from Pushkin. *"Ya pil—i gorye zhizni skorotechnoi i sni lyubvi vospominal."* As my poet-mentor said: I drank—and then recalled the bitterness of fleeting life, the dreams of love.

I was giving it a second rendition as a kind of Mozartean recitative, *molto spiritoso,* when a large figure loomed out of the fog. No, he was standing still, it was *I* who did the looming. Swaying, in any case. Whatever the first impression, it was soon obvious that this apparition, a tall, broad man like a square-shouldered and squarer-jawed Michael Caine, with a military haircut and a marine's aggressive stance, was standing in the middle of the pavement, refusing to move. Like Pushkin's statue of Peter the Great, his immobility threatened more convincingly than any action he might have taken.

I stopped, steadied myself, looked him up and down and debated whether to make an issue of his monopoly of the pavement, go around him by stepping out onto the street, or turn tail and retreat to the café. The debate was short. I did a zagged about turn and retreated to the café.

"Rond comme un coing," I heard him say with a laugh.

Though how the shape of a quince came to describe my mildly . . . fuzzy condition, God only knew.

I put out a hand to the glass-paneled café door and turned the handle. Inside Pierre was talking to someone, not the elderly *patron,* another man, with red hair. Michel? Good. But Pierre was looking anxious. Red hair? There was something familiar . . . Was the wine . . . ?

The back of my coat collar gave a sudden jerk. I swung—reeled—around.

I opened my mouth to protest. A fist hit it. I fell against the glass door. Vaguely, inside, I saw Pierre jump up. I was spinning. There were two men, three. One still held my collar. The redhead was grabbing Pierre. The third it was, outside the café, who slugged me. On the left temple with a blackjack. I took a nose dive into the fog and never came up.

Not until, that's to say, I awoke in the back of that Renault van, surrounded by feet and the butts of submachine guns . . . .

Chapter 4

December 15.   Pre-dawn.

"Not worth a rabbit's fart," the sergeant-major shouted as the de-bussing began, "all those rules and regulations, safety precautions. You can't stop a good hijack. Okay, you stay there, Ivan. Get out, Number Four. Make it quick! Those shit-shovelers think it'll never happen. They aren't ready for it. Point a gun at 'em and you'll see their asses tighten. Incompetents. Fall on their backs and they break their noses."

"Speaks the lingo like a bloody Spanish cow, don't 'e?" the Cockney said, nudging me on his way out of the back of the van.

"Calls hisself the sergeant-major."

"Oh! He does?"

So I'd been right about one thing—how to characterize the big man.

"Yeah. Ta-ra, mate."

"Get out there now," the sergeant-major snapped, pulling the Cockney by the arm. "And keep quiet." Then, to me: "Okay, Bolcho, shove back up in there and shut up. I've got other cats to whip."

"Go bomb yourself," I thought, but didn't say.

I climbed back into the van. The door slammed shut. The large flashlight that had been strapped to the handle fell off. The feeble light it had provided died instantly. Outside, a bolt screeched into place.

I brooded.

There was still alcohol in my thoughts, it guided me back toward the Auberge du Vieux Port, then toward that desolate café in Beaumont. So long ago. Were the film crew now around at the *gendarmerie,* complaining about their yacht and the old man's power-boat fantasies? Was Mackeson-Beadle with them, in jail maybe? No, he'd gone off somewhere. Where? I couldn't remember. Then I remembered that I didn't know. That was the whole point.

But the old man's fears about Ronnie hadn't been wrong. Well, they hadn't been wild *enough,* that was the problem. Sir Ronald—unless I was caught up in some weird coincidence—was for real. Mad perhaps, but not incapable of doing what he raved. I had seriously underestimated the man.

And those guys out there, they had to be Ronnie Hisland's private army, his personal, private *force de frappe.* But was their object really just to show how lax security was at the French plutonium plant? I mean, did they need submachine guns to make that point? It was perplexing.

Amanda! The image erupted again in my mind. Wasn't I meant to be meeting her somewhere? I groaned. She'd never believe me! Of course I should have told her what it was we were doing in France. Maybe she'd have been some help. Still, I didn't put it past her to organize a one-woman search. I would never have thought I'd welcome the role of escaped lover pursued by a furious woman but at the moment the idea had its attractions. She was intrepid enough to succeed. I mean, that was one of her attractive qualities. She was no quitter. She was full not of feminine-wiles bullshit but of honest British bulldog tenacity. Except the bull-dog image was a bit too accurate . . . .

Meanwhile, however, the *force de frappe* was a more immediate threat. They were ominously well prepared, well organized. And if they were hunting for a black-mail weapon, they were pursuing the most dangerous game of all. Because that's what plutonium is, the world's most potent blackmail weapon. Everyone has heard about the perils of plutonium. A chemical like Dioxan may be more potent; it kills in parts per trillion, not parts per million. But it still doesn't give the authorities that *frisson* they feel when plutonium is the weapon. The public too. No politician or policeman (and in France what's the difference?) can risk out-bluffing a criminal with plutonium. You can juggle with the lives of a hundred hostages, take risks to get them back, even pretend to give way to the criminals' demands, as long as they're not too outrageous. But you can't risk the lives of hundreds of thousands, millions, of people.

Nuclear blackmail is the easiest to decide how to deal with—it's pay up every time.

I thought about that time when the Israelis rescued the Air France passengers from Entebbe Airport, sent in commandos, shot up the hijackers and got out again. They could never have done that if instead of just human beings there'd been plutonium in the airport building. Impossible. If the hijackers had primed the plutonium so as to make it critical just by bringing two lumps together or by a simple TNT explosion, they would have let it off at the first shot.

Meanwhile—God!—my head hurt!

Sir Ronald! Christ! It was hard to follow through any consistent line of thought about him. Of course I'd imagined him as a crackpot, an old buffer who, because he had the sort of money that few of his fellow-pensioners reduced to living in Bexhill and Bournemouth ever dreamed of, had slid off into a world where he no longer distinguished between fantasy and acting out his fantasies. But what did he need to prove to Mackeson-Beadle? The Tweedledum theory was all right as far as it went, which wasn't far. Okay, Ronnie Hisland was a frustrated military man, obliged to work out the end of his career on the fringes of soldiering as a diplomat, a military attaché. It was reasonable to assume he now wanted some action, even if he had to start the war himself. But that didn't mean his mind had gone completely. He surely didn't imagine himself as some Christian Yassir Arafat, or anti-"Che" Guevara, or "Carlos" . . . only converted, like St. Paul, to the other side. No. He wasn't even the classic loony figure of a reincarnated Napoleon. He was plain Sir Ronald Hisland and had to be understood as such.

Even at this pre-dawn hour, when reality and unreality were hard to tell apart and thoughts took flight of their own accord, Sir Ronald Hisland was in no danger of being mistaken for a dream.

Outside, as if to prove the point, the sergeant-major barked an order.

An assortment of moans and groans followed, mostly to do with the rain, still coming down like a pissing cow.

Does it rain on soldiers more than on other people? It would seem so. I remembered the permanent puddle sloshing around in my Red army tank and thinking I might just as well have joined the Navy. In 1956 I'd have been much better off—at least they didn't send sailors into Budapest.

But what was I doing now, sitting here in a semi-daze, just thinking? There must be something I could *do*.

It was safer being imprisoned than on the firing line. All the same, now, I wanted at least to know what was going on.

So I fumbled around the back of the van—not to test the bolt because I'd heard it shut securely; and besides I had no intention of disobeying orders by getting out. I was looking for any holes or slits through which I could *see* out. As if in answer to a silent prayer my fingers touched a movable metal panel separating the cab from the back compartment where I was, a small window covered by a sliding shutter. It was pulled across, but not locked. My fingertips gripped its protruding edge and I pulled with a gentle but gradually increasing pressure until I felt something slide. A dim, very dim light indeed filtered into my *cachette*.

As my eyes adjusted, what I first saw was the back of a head, masked and anonymous.

The person was bent over reading a map by the

source of the light, a slim penlight. I noticed beside him on the bench seat a piece of equipment that looked like a shortwave radio but which on more intense inspection turned out to be a walkie-talkie, the same kind as I'd seen in the yellow dinghy at Diélette.

Then another head shot across from the right, bursting into my restricted line of vision, the large round head of Sir Ronald Hisland. The van swayed slightly. It was good to see him, to know he was there, that it wasn't *my* fantasy he was acting out!

All the same, it was a strange sensation, a strange view of things I had, as if I were in a movie studio viewing the rushes of a Candid Camera production; or was this how a bank security officer felt, watching the images packed into a small screen by a single fixed television camera out front?

In any case I had an extra problem. Either I could watch what was going on, or I could twist my ear to the tiny opening to listen. Not both at the same time.

They seemed to be talking up there in the cab, a faint mumble. I made sure I could see nothing beyond the dashboard and windshield and decided that the best choice was to listen. I applied my ear.

"Just under an hour, then," I could make out Sir Ronald saying. "Time you set off?"

"Another five minutes, sir."

A pause. Then:

"Where's the bike, eh?"

"Round the corner, sir. As arranged."

A longish silence was broken by Sir Ronald again. "Sergeant-major's got everyone posted, I hope. Er, recap, eh?"

Ronnie seemed to feel the need to keep talking. It wasn't surprising he was getting pre-action nerves.

84

"Convoy due at the N804-D22 crossroads at 0745 hours," he went on. "Right. Soon as you spot 'em, you send the signal. Then pedal down and get into position. Here!"

His finger made a snap as it stabbed the map.

"Last junction before the bridge. Cut off their retreat, eh? Not, by God, that there'll be any retreating. I checked the timing again on the way and it shouldn't be more than four and a half minutes from the crossroads to the bridge here. That's the slowest. Gives us an ETA of 0749 and a half. Max."

"Dawn's at 0815. Can't wait beyond that. No way."

"That should do it. Half an hour's grace. Action at last, eh? I'll listen out for you. Check your arrival once in position."

The bang of the cab door zinged through the metal and into my eardrum. I jerked my head away, then, cautiously, risked another look. Sir Ronald sat alone in front now. I could only just discern the silhouette of his face in the absence of the flashlight, but now and again a faint red glow from the bowl of his pipe lit up his heavy features. He sat motionless. I too kept still, not wanting to remind him that I was behind him. Nor did I want to reveal that I had a line of view into the cab and, perhaps, if there were any sunlight, a view beyond.

Suddenly the noise of an explosion made me flinch backward.

The black night erupted with a metallic roar. Sparks spat like fireworks and a flash of brilliance flared up in a fulminating climax . . . I flung myself back to the spy hole. As I got there the light gradually faded . . . faded.

A train. A mere train. It banged by and away along the embankment, almost directly over my head. The shell shock subsided into a thumping heartbeat.

The train's headlights and sparks had, however, done something to make up for the fright they gave me. They had momentarily showed me where we were.

The van was parked up against a steeply angled slope leading to the railway track, five yards back from a mainish road along a smaller, though asphalted, road leading to Couville station. A sign reading GARE DE COUVILLE 0,3 had imprinted itself on my mind as the train flashed by. More significantly, the scrubby embankment was pierced where it hit the road in front of me by an oblong black hole in a brick arch. Sir Ronald's bridge. It looked, so far as my brief perspective could be trusted, remarkably narrow.

Their plan was beginning to become more comprehensible. A classic ambush. But what would be traveling by road? One of the *châteaux,* maybe. Ronnie'd mentioned a convoy. So had the sergeant-major. Did they mean a long line of trucks? Or a single truck and its escort? Or . . . I tried to remember what I knew about the dangerous materials that go in and out of a plutonium reprocessing plant. Spent fuel in . . . and coming out, the plutonium itself.

It would all depend on which way the truck or convoy was traveling. It was coming from a crossroads. I'd overheard the map reference but that told me nothing. If from right to left, toward La Hague, it would probably be the spent fuel. The other way . . . something much more dangerous.

Meanwhile across the road that passed under the bridge, a little way up a rough path, I thought I saw a white Simca. Of Ronnie's men there was no sign. They must already be in ambush positions.

No other traffic disturbed the peace or gave me another view of the battleground. Nothing at all along the

86

road, either way. Maybe a milk truck would begin its rounds, collecting the cans at the end of lanes and paths —surely they must be collected or dumped or whatever early in the morning? It would be a real foul-up of Ronnie's plans if one happened along at just the right moment . . .

But before dawn? It was too much to hope for. The smile on my face faded.

Then the shadow in the cab moved, and I put my ear back to the metal partition.

The walkie-talkie was crackling. I heard something coming through the static and Sir Ronald making an indistinct reply. Whatever the exact words, the man who'd been with him in the cab was apparently in position.

I glanced at my watch. The luminosity of the hands was wearing out, but in the extreme blackness where I sat there was just enough radioactive green to make out either twenty-three to four or seventeen after seven. The second reading was obviously correct—still more than half an hour to the action predicted at seven-fifty. They weren't taking any chances about the convoy coming by early. I tried to adjust my bones for the wait without giving up my vantage point or making a clatter. A kind of kneeling crouch worked best.

Seven-thirty.

Forty . . . forty-five . . . fifty. Ah hah! The convoy was late. Canceled . . . ? Had they got word, suspected something?

Sir Ronald shifted in the cab, fiddling with the walkie-talkie. There was some under-the-breath swearing, some of it reaching my ear.

But no signal.

Yet.

Then a faint beam of light flashed into my peephole.

I put my head up and looked through. The wet surface of the road in front of the bridge flickered in the light of the headlights from a vehicle far back up the road. Ronnie Hisland called up someone on his walkie-talkie. Nothing. He shouted angrily.

"Come in! D'you hear me? Come in, man."

He fumbled some more with the buttons on the side of the instrument, damning it and blasting it. There was a crackling noise like asbestos in a fire.

"What? Eh? No?"

Then to himself: "If those buggers have chosen a different route . . ."

I put my head up and saw him scrabbling about with his map. The beam of his flashlight, slightly fatter than the other one, made spidery patterns all over it, tracing the roads which the convoy could possibly have taken to reach the bridge without having to pass through the crossroads where the man was waiting to give an advance warning. Sir Ronald must have judged it possible, because he pointed the beam up and out through the windshield, flashing it on, off, then on again.

The yellow light piercing the bridge from the left grew stronger through the rain-smeared windshield in front of me.

From the left! Leaving La Hague. Not spent fuel, then. Plutonium!

Suddenly two headlights directly in front of me glared into my eyes through the streaks and spots on the glass screen. The car parked opposite pulled out, nosing forward tentatively, as if about to turn to its right under the bridge.

On my left, I heard a honk from the other vehicle approaching the narrow tunnel of the bridge. Then, in seconds, a squeal of brakes. Almost at once the nose of a truck shot out from under the bridge into my line of vision. It pulled up inches short of the Simca's front fender.

Again, its horn blared.

I held my breath, waiting for the attack.

But no one moved. No one except the driver of the truck, in silhouette, gesturing obscenities.

The Simca backed up the path. A shout penetrated my prison . . . abuse, something about someone's sister. The truck ground angrily into first gear and drove on.

As the back of it emerged from the tunnel under the railway line in front of me, I saw a picture painted on its side. The outline of a Norman cow. In the flickering light, the cow, bespectacled and benign, seemed to wink. *La vache qui rit!* I winked back. You nearly fouled it up, cow! You did your best!

But now, as soon as the milk truck disappeared into the night, the Simca's lights went out and my little vista went black.

I felt a sudden letdown, like Gilbert Pradal, perhaps, after the final "cut." But in fact the camera kept turning. The action didn't stop. The big scene just had to be reshot.

Sir Ronald immediately clambered down from his seat in the Renault van. My pupils had dilated again by the time he'd crossed the road, and I saw him begin an angry exchange with the driver of the Simca. Then he ran back to his HQ and observation post in the cab, pulled himself up and started fiddling again with the walkie-talkie.

Why, oh why, does every single military action in which I'm involved, even as a mere spectator, always turn into a shambles?

Irene, goddess of peace, watches over me.

Well, it wasn't a shambles altogether, yet. Perhaps a foretaste. At all events I felt cheered. And it was already seven-fifty-five. I laughed silently. The passing of time meant only one thing: an increasing chance that word had got out there was something afoot; an increasing chance that the nuclear convoy had, after all, been stopped. For me, each second of delay was a sign of hope.

For the others, it was like playing on their nerves with a frayed bowstring. I wondered if even the sergeant-major was being affected, somewhere out there in the pre-dawn black?

EIGHT O'CLOCK, two past . . . five past.

Not even the rain falling steadily from the black clouds overhead could blot out altogether the first glimmering of the unrisen but approaching sun. False dawn. Second by second, minute by minute, outlines emerged, became sharper, the trees first, patterns of twigs in the faintest tracery. Two roadsigns, black letters on a white background, just across the road by the path up which the Simca was parked became my touchstone of the advancing and real dawn.

By seven minutes after eight I could make them out despite the rain on the van's windshield. The lefthand one said 6 TEURTHEVILLE-HAGUE, the one on its right ST. MARTIN-LE GRÉARD I,6.

Then slogans in chalk or whitewash emanated like letters in lemon juice held up to the fire from the red brick walls of the bridge, until I could read a couple of them with clarity. LAIT 73 and VIANDE 10,50—prices demanded by the *agriculteurs* of the Cotentin, long since vitiated by inflation.

Eight-ten.

Now only five minutes to official dawn. That was the cut-off point. Surely Sir Ronald Hisland was not going to risk a hijack by daylight.

As for the sergeant-major—I had an urge to gloat in his face about the increasingly desperate situation he was in, to ask him how it felt now, skating on soggy cabbage . . . .

But not too soon.

It wasn't time yet. Not quite . . . .

Still there was no traffic, nothing since the milk truck. Then the walkie-talkie crackled again.

Ronnie Hisland sprang out of what seemed to be a trance. "Yes? Yes?" he yelled into his handset as if it were a tin can joined by a piece of string to the other end. "Roger!"

With his ear still clamped to the receiver, he started blinking his flashlight across at the waiting Simca, the same signal, twice . . . three times. Then he put down the torch and turned on the van's windshield wipers. Suddenly, for the first time, everything came into focus, foiling the rain's persistent attempt to distort what little I could see through my narrow screen.

We waited . . . another minute. Two.

Then, once again, the flicker of distant yellow headlights began to play through the black hole of the bridge . . . brighter. Again, Sir Ronald waited with his flashlight, then flashed another triple signal. The Simca's headlights flared. It pulled out . . . A horn blared.

Take two.

This time it was for real.

THE FRONT of the big Berliet truck slammed the right front fender of the Simca, slewed it around, metal screaming, gouging the brick on the tunnel's inner walls. A burst of gunfire crackled from the far side of the bridge. Two masked men leaped from their concealed positions on top of the bridge, landing on the roof of the cab. One lost his footing and clutched at the side mirror, swayed, overbalanced.

I watched the *danse macabre* on the puppet-stage in front of me, spellbound. There were two men in the cab, two men on the roof. One inside was armed, on the far side of the driver as I saw it. Beyond him, clutching and sliding, appeared the head and torso of the hijacker. The guard drew what appeared to be a handgun and fired two shots at this upside-down apparition beside him. The hijacker's body jerked back and away, as if springing down from the truck. But the guard would have done better to follow the example of the truck driver who sat rigid, his hands above his head, his fear-frozen eyes staring straight ahead. His companion was the victim of his well-conditioned reflexes. The second hijacker fired immediately through the driver's window into the head and body of the guard.

The cab suddenly filled with blood and red splintered glass. Thank God the surviving hijacker slid down from the roof and blocked my view.

Behind the bridge, a crash of glass and metal echoed the Berliet's fate. The hollower bang of an exploding tire . . . a flash . . . shouts, a confused pattering like the drum of rain.

Suddenly there seemed to be a swarm of masked men.

Then silence. So soon.

The firing stopped. The muscles in the back of my neck relaxed and I pulled away from the viewing panel, realizing my forehead was pressed painfully against the glass.

Sir Ronald Hisland had been as transfixed, as immobile, as myself. Now the brief, violent action was over. He stirred, shook his head, realized it had all happened. It was over. He had to go and check the results, organize the next stage, take command.

At that moment, the largest of the masked figures—the sergeant-major, surely—came running through the narrow gap between the stalled plutonium truck and the bridge. Sir Ronald Hisland, lowering himself from the Renault cab, conferred briefly with him. Then other men came up, ran off. The big man pulled his mask back over his head, reminding me miserably of our first meeting in fogbound Beaumont. A tough, good-looking soldier—cocky bastard!

The two dead men, one guard and one hijacker, were ignored by all the survivors. The driver who had so prudently surrendered was nowhere I could see.

Now it was a question of unloading and reloading. As rapidly as possible.

If there had been an escort car, it had been dealt with further back up the road as efficiently as the men in the Berliet truck.

No, it wasn't a shambles at all but a carefully planned and well-executed operation. The guards had been overwhelmed by superior firepower and numbers at a place where they had no chance to make a run for it and no time to fight back.

A click. Light flooded into the back of my van. I hadn't been taking it in, how fast the dawn had come up.

The sergeant-major's face appeared. "Butter!" he said, stabbing a finger in my direction. "Not a fucking *hic!* Okay, Russko, out! No room for you *and* the other stuff in there. Unless you want to keep it company."

I piled out.

"What've you got in there?" I asked, pointing my own finger at the truck. My hand was shaking.

The sergeant-major smiled. "It sure isn't soap powder."

"Plutonium?"

"Spot on. Now move."

I had no reason to disbelieve him. Every reason to take him at his word. Things couldn't have turned out worse. Did Ronnie realize, though, what he was messing with? This plutonium stuff from the plant was the deadliest of all the materials he could possibly have gotten hold of. I felt sick. Fear, the lack of food, that revolting scene in the truck cab . . . it was all combining. I looked up at the sky, more to distract myself than in prayer. It worked, and the nausea subsided.

The light was far stronger. Even though it was—just —more night than day; when, as the French say, you can't tell a dog from a wolf. The rain fell steadily. I let it trickle down my face.

Three masked men ran up.

"Slung both the buggers in the ditch," the Cockney said to the sergeant-major. "Car's okay. Bit of bother getting one of 'em out the door. That's all. Charl— . . . Number Four, he got it off the road."

"Okay. *Allez!* Get those asses of your shifting!"

The truck, an unmarked Berliet three-tonner, ground out from under the bridge, and I had to shift my own ass as it reversed toward the station, turned and pointed its back at the back of the Renault.

It needed nerve to drive it. The body of the dead guard was inside, slumped bloodily against the shat-

94

tered windshield. I looked away, but the nausea was back.

They made me stand on the other side of the road under the watchful eye of a man on the embankment beside the railway line. From there he was able to observe not only the two houses close by—both about a hundred yards away and no lights showing through the rain—but also the road on both sides of the bridge . . . and me.

I still hoped for a snag when it came to transferring the plutonium. Some *hic* that would delay the operation, give the police time to wake up and come after them. Radio contact was ordered to be almost continuous, wasn't it? How long did that really give them? Five minutes, maybe?

But the transfer turned out to be rapid and easy. Either by design or accident, the tailgate of the Berliet truck made a chute down which four metal objects, about a meter by a meter and a half, were simply slid like beer kegs into a pub cellar.

What surprised me most was that the containers weren't solid at all. I don't know why but I'd imagined a battery of upended steamer trunks with their silver linings showing, rather like Mackeson-Beadle's "bar," only inside out. Instead they were hollow steel cages. Each of the six sides consisted of an X of steel bars from which spokes protruded inward, holding in the center a canister like a blunt-nosed artillery shell. Inside these steel cylinders, padlocked and bolted, were the tin cans, or bottles, of plutonium.

Four of these pieces of modern sculpture, primed with their deadly centers, were packed neatly into the Renault troop-carrier. The rest were abandoned in the truck.

The loading was over. Two figures, still masked, dragged off the dead body of their comrade killed by the guard in the Berliet cab. His rubber boots slid noiselessly across the smooth tarmac. They bundled him unceremoniously into the back of the truck with the rest of the plutonium. No harm in contaminating a corpse!

I was so absorbed by watching these operations that I hadn't noticed Sir Ronald Hisland come up beside me. He too, like the sergeant-major, couldn't suppress a grin.

"We've made it, you see, Gull. Only lost one. Not one of the best. Rogue, in fact. That's life, isn't it?"

I said nothing, but he was too stimulated to stop talking.

"Didn't think an old buffer like me could do it, did you? Thought I was batty. Ha-ha."

He laughed like a music-hall villain and waved a heavy pistol as if to prove he was a real hunter, not an armchair safari. A raindrop glistened on his florid nose.

"Awkward customer, aren't you, Gull? That drug I gave you wore off too soon. Sergeant-major was right, I suppose. You were meant to sleep through the op, you see."

"A silent hostage. Just in case."

"Ha-ha. Quite so."

He caught me staring at the heavy pistol he was holding in his right hand.

"It's German. Jerries left a pile of stuff behind on the Islands. I keep it well oiled. Sergeant-major calls it a 'jolly *tac-tac*.' Ha-ha. I'd use it too."

"Sir Jasper," I said, "remind me to hiss."

He glared at me. "You're a fool and a cynic, Gull. Let me tell you two things you don't understand. First,

96

timing. This whole op is timed to a T. Even my loud-mouthing to old Godfrey hasn't upset it one jot. No, not even your coming over here. God, the sergeant-major said you were *drunk!* Drunk on duty! Not me—not us. Dawn raid. Copy book. In . . ."—he consulted his wrist-watch—" . . . in exactly two hours and a half, plus ten minutes for transport, we load up and away out of the country. In four and three quarter hours, subject to minor adjustments for weather, the plutonium will be where I want it. Now, what's the other thing? I said two. Ah yes, teamwork. You saw it in action. Fine chap, the sergeant-major, runs the whole show."

"He told me. Several times."

"I'll be sorry to see him go."

"Go?"

"Of course. Once this op's over, I'll be on my own for the next stage. This is just the military part. At eleven this morning we enter the political stage, which'll be more interesting to you, Gull, I imagine?"

"Maybe. What are you going to do with the plutonium?"

Part of me wanted to ask what *my* fate was going to be, but I had a feeling he hadn't made up his mind yet and I didn't want him to rush into words and find himself obstinately committed to the first solution that came to mind.

In either case Ronnie was uninformative. "Never mind, young man," was all he said.

"You've already proved your point," I prompted him. "Plutonium can be stolen. Big deal. Anyone can play cowboys and Indians if they're crazy enough."

He reddened. "When you see I'm not playing games, you'll—"

"I've seen enough already," I replied sharply. "What

fascinates me is what you're going to do when you
finally find out what's *really* inside there."

I stabbed a finger at the cages that held the transferred plutonium.

"Eh?"

I just looked at him. Then I grinned.

"What d'you mean?" he repeated.

"Check."

Sir Ronald hesitated. Would he take my remark seriously enough to examine the containers more closely?
Here and now? Any delay could be critical.

"Nonsense, Gull. What d'you mean?"

I didn't know what I was talking about, but I could
improvise. It was an impulse. Would he detail a man to
check? Maybe.

"They're dummies," I said. "Pierre told me."

"Denis?" He pronounced it to rhyme with menace.
"If that little . . . ."

He was wavering. I was ready to press my advantage,
at the very least distract him, get him talking about
Pierre, anything, but the sergeant-major cut the ground
from under me. He appeared from nowhere and stood
between me and Sir Ronald.

"If that piss-artist's finished, sir, we're ready to move
off."

"Right," said Sir Ronald firmly, glancing scornfully
in my direction. "Let's get weaving!"

I TRIED to persist but the sergeant-major wasn't having
any. He pushed me into the back of the Simca and
crammed himself in beside me. My other neighbor
snatched off his rain-beaded mask, revealing himself as
the redhead, now also red-stubbled and red-eyed. He

98

glowered at me, half triumphantly and half, I felt, in dazed bewilderment. Had *he* fired the shot that killed the guard?

The trunk lid slammed shut.

Behind, the plutonium truck—minus four containers, although the hijacker's body had taken their place—ground into life, moved off right and headed toward St. Martin-Le Gréard. One man was in the cab.

The Renault van, the four cages of plutonium in the back, started up. The Cockney was driving. It turned left under the bridge, back in the direction of the sign to Teurtheville-Hague.

At the same time Sir Ronald climbed into the Simca, up front beside the driver. The engine was already running.

"Put that gun down on the floor, lad," the sergeant-major said sharply to the red-haired man on my other side. "And take it easy."

The man slouched self-consciously back in his seat. "I'm getting out in half a second, ain't I?" he said sullenly.

"We ready, then?" That was the driver. I could identify him for the first time, a small, wispy-haired, pinched-faced man in his twenties.

"Carry on!" barked Commandant Hisland.

The car moved off fast, following the van. Not more than two minutes had elapsed since the loading operation began, four since the final shot had been fired. Like a Royal Command Performance. Or was I thinking of the Royal Tournament? Smooth, efficient, in any case.

Once we'd negotiated the bridge, I saw what had happened to the escort car and its occupants. A silver-gray Peugeot 505 was parked in a narrow lane on the left, fifty yards beyond the railway bridge. Its windshield was also shattered, and its two front tires were flat.

On the corner of the lane, behind a pair of milk cans, a man's leg stuck up from a ditch. It was a momentary impression, nothing more. All I could see.

A hundred yards farther on we stopped to pick up the lookout who was standing casually beside the bike, as if he'd had an easy battle. He had. There'd been no retreat. The red-haired man got out, took the bicycle and pedaled off into the dawn. In his blue workclothes he merged into the landscape like a Millet peasant.

I was too intent staring at the lookout to see the girl until the lookout, a thinner, older version of the sergeant-major, pointed her out.

"Bird," he said simply. "In the back of the escort car. Says she knows about plutonium and all, expert sort of lady. We thought she would be useful."

"Good man," said Sir Ronald out of the car window. "Get her in here and we'll have a chat as we go. There's room if we squeeze up tight. Ha-ha!"

She was sitting on the bank. A well-made woman on a delicate, continental scale, very blonde as I could see from hair escaping the fur-lined hood of a wine-colored suede coat. The coat, incidentally, was the worse for wear after the treatment dealt out to the escort car and five minutes in the freezing rain and mud. Her cheeks, mildly disfigured by a bruise rising below her right eye, had a patina of pale down.

Prompted by the lookout, she finally got to her feet . . . and staggered. Maybe she'd been injured, or maybe her foot had just gone to sleep? In either case, the sergeant-major was unsympathetic. He rolled down the window and snarled, *"Allez! Debout, ma cocotte!* Up!"

Then, to the lookout: "Hold her up. Can't have mademoiselle falling in the apples!"

The driver giggled.

Sir Ronald stepped out and held the door for her, gallant to a fault. She pushed into the gap between the front seats and made herself as comfortable as she could in a car with bucket seats and a stick shift. The hood fell back onto her shoulders revealing the full head of blonde hair piled precariously, ready to unravel voluptuously with the simple stunning gesture of removing a comb and tossing the head. No, no. My imagination was running away with me. In point of fact her hair was a mess, snarled and spiked by snapped-off bramble twigs.

The lookout jumped in the back where the redhead had been, and the car lurched off again. It was getting like some college fraternity stunt—how many people can you cram into . . . whatever.

"Name?" Sir Ronald barked, gallantry forgotten.

"Hein?"

"No bloody English. Typical. I might have guessed. The French never can learn a civilized language. Ask her, sergeant-major."

"What do they call you?" he said, in his highly personalized French accent.

"Bonnissent. Sophie!"

"Bonney-sent, sir," he translated. "Smells nice. Common enough Norman name," he added.

She raised her eyes, and we looked at each other in the rear mirror. I smiled conspiratorially. She looked away. She wasn't going to strike up any understanding with a hijacker.

Sir Ronald was applying a match to shreds of ash deep inside his briar, so I piped up from the back, again, of course, in French. "My name's Vladimir Gull. I'm like you, along for the ride. You don't have to tell the bastards anything."

"That'll do, Gull, whatever you're telling her!" Sir Ronald exploded.

She turned to look at me properly this time and smiled back—what a blue-eyed smile!

"They're playing soldiers," I went on. "Just give them your name, rank and serial number."

"Thank you," she said, "but I think I can handle them."

"Okay, but these *merdeurs* . . . ."

On cue, the sergeant-major rammed me in the ribs with his angular elbow, hard as reinforced concrete. But I'd wanted to make a gesture of prisoners' solidarity. In unity there is strength. An injury to one is an injury to all.

"Ask her what she was doing, sergeant-major, in that escort car."

The sergeant-major did as he was bid, but clumsily. Sophie Bonnissent pretended not to understand. As a device, if it was a device, it wasn't bad. I had a better idea.

"You clearly need a professional interpreter, commandant," I said to Ronnie. "That's my job, as you well know. Your sergeant-major can listen in and check."

I didn't want to make things more difficult for the young woman, but I knew just how important a figure an interpreter can be. There are tiny changes he can slip in, information he can leave out, or add or turn into misinformation, which only the most expert can detect. This could be useful if she actually was a nuclear expert. But the real reason I volunteered was something else. I needed a role. I was feeling dangerously dispensable, especially after witnessing the hijack and the shootings.

The sergeant-major and his commandant checked each others' eye signals and seemed willing to accept the proposition. So I took over and asked her what she'd been doing.

"Monitoring the plutonium," she said, and I translated.

"Monitoring?" asked Sir Ronald.

She nodded. "Seeing it doesn't get too hot, doing routine checks, then supervising the unloading in Paris."

"Ha! Then you're just the lady we need! Well thought of indeed, brother George."

"Brother George?" I couldn't help asking.

"Ah yes, sergeant-major's brother. Our lookout man."

"Georges," said the man—insisting on the French pronunciation.

Georges stared out the window, not enjoying this distribution of free information. I wasn't sure it helped me either. In the long run, the less I knew the better— or maybe I already knew so damn much it didn't matter any more.

An angel passed. Silence, except for the squish of tires on the muddy lane that jumped into prominence as we drove fast and west across the Cotentin, like the last stragglers bombing homeward after an all-night party.

Seconds later came a hitch, a *hic* as the sergeant-major would say.

On the far side of Couville-Village a herd of brown-spotted Norman cows like the one pictured on the side of the milk truck that had so nearly put an end to the operation was taking advantage of the first light to waddle from pasture to milking shed. A figure of indeterminate sex in a long brown overcoat and fisherman's oilskin hat waved a stick desultorily but with minimum effect.

The Simca skidded as the tires locked, then slammed to a dead stop. The Renault van appeared directly in front of us. It had also been brought to a halt by the cows.

Sir Ronald looked at his watch and swore.

I looked at mine and smiled.

Far in the distance a police siren wailed. Had the alert been sounded? How much longer before the whole area was swarming with *flics?*

The sergeant-major stared at me—at me looking at the door-catches beside the back seat of the Simca. He shook his head silently. His own submachine gun might be clumsy to use in our cramped quarters, but I was the pâté in the sandwich; the two brothers were the bread, crusty and time-hardened. I didn't want to give them an excuse to spread me any thinner between them.

So far the delays and diversions had all occurred before the hijacking, a total, frustrating waste as things turned out. Now I wanted some real luck.

Were these cows it?

We waited, crawled forward, stopped.

Everyone now was fidgeting, scowling, except me and Sophie Bonnissent, who was keeping her cool remarkably well.

The cows slopped on slowly down the narrow road, adding their excrement to the surface already slippery with rain and mud.

Another siren . . . the knell of rising day? Then silence, a solemn stillness.

We advanced another five yards. Stopped.

I was beginning to feel hopeful again, when, from lazy habit, the mastodonic brown-and-white beasts began to turn into a gap in a high granite wall beside the road and lumber into a gray stone barn. The drover didn't even turn to look at the Renault van and the Simca held up by his troupe. Just for a moment I thought something could come out of this holdup, that we might at least have a witness. But no. The last cow vanished through the hole in the wall. The Renault van accelerated away and out of sight. Seconds later we took a left turn onto a separate route. Neither vehicle had been noticed.

So that was it. The operation over . . . and successful. Sir Ronald Hisland sighed with relief, smiled contentedly and lit a pipe. The old soldier after battle.

A battle he had good reason to believe he had won.

"NOW WHERE?" I asked.

No one answered.

Catching Miss Bonnissent's eye again in the mirror, I thought of Amanda. A ridiculous connection to make, but perhaps inevitable. What *had* happened to her? Or her father? Had she just turned around and gone back to England? Possible but unlikely. And Pierre? They must have picked him up in Beaumont. The sergeant-major had more or less admitted he was under guard. Where? And why had they brought me along but not him? These were gaps in my knowledge I'd probably need patience to fill.

I felt a surge of hunger. God, I'd swallowed nothing but surplus adrenaline since that rotgut in the Beaumont café! Unless they'd administered the drug orally.

Another police siren . . . but more distant than the first.

What the hell were they *doing* out there?

Sir Ronald Hisland twisted around in the front seat of the Simca and looked at me. "Hear that, Gull? Quick off the mark. Quicker than I expected. But going the other way, aren't they? Ha-ha. Soon find the lorry. That'll have 'em guessing."

"And looking some more."

He dismissed the idea with a wave of his hand.

"Not so fast, driver. Don't want to get arrested for speeding."

He laughed again. Not much more than a chuckle this time. A sign on which the name BENOITVILLE was slashed by a diagonal red line indicated we had just passed through that village. But it was hard to tell one huddle of gray stone houses and barns from another. Besides, I hardly knew the countryside around here. I might have seen it from the air when I'd flown from Cherbourg to Guernsey if it hadn't been for the low clouds. Even so, what use would that have been to me now? None.

Sir Ronald twisted his head around.

"Must show you today's edition of the *Post,*" he said. "The communiqué's in. Or should be."

"*Post?* Communiqué?"

"Yes, yes, man. Guernsey *Evening Post.* Clever ploy. A pity I have to set up Godfrey as the leading light. Makes it seem as if the old boy has gone barmy, of course, but that just makes 'em sit up and take notice. Nothing more dangerous than a lunatic loose with all that plutonium, eh? Unless it's someone who knows damn well what they're doing," he added sharply.

I tried to sort it out from the beginning. "Just what will be in the paper?" I asked. "An ad in the buy-and-sell column?"

"Oh, what you'd expect, Gull," Sir Ronald replied in

an offhand way. "Enough to show 'em we mean business in the FGM."

"FGM?"

"Good God, Gull, don't you know about the Free Guernsey Movement? The FGM?" He paused. "No, of course you don't. How could you? But you will. I've made sure they'll hear of it from Cornwall to the bloody Shetlands. And in Dodge City, Wollongong and every other tinpot place in every corner of the whole bloody world."

He glared at me over his shoulder. "FGM'll push the Palestinians off the front pages. That's my object. Oh yes, it'll happen. In time."

Brother Georges beside me started humming the tune to that Gilbert and Sullivan song, "My object all sublime I shall achieve in time—to let the punishment fit the crime, the punishment fit the crime," realized what he was doing and shut up in mid-flow. Even so, it struck me as oddly insubordinate.

Meanwhile, I wondered what the hell Ronnie meant by setting up Mackeson-Beadle as the "leading light" of the FGM. Had Amanda's old dad hightailed it back to Guernsey then? Even the Island Police Force wouldn't have a problem winkling him out if he had, not once his name appeared in the *Post*. But *how* did Godfrey's "chum" plan to pin the theft on him? I knew I should encourage Ronnie to keep talking.

"Independence," he started up again without needing me as prompter. "Independence. It's the modern thing, isn't it? Even those Corsican fellows are doing it. Chaps in the Isle of Man burn down the houses when foreigners move in, but they've got it wrong. National pride, sovereignty—baloney! It's money. Money. That's what counts. I'm damned if my island is going to go broke just because the socialists are throwing out the good old days on the mainland. Out of sheer envy and spite, mark you. It's a simple choice. The good life on our own. Or a neglected corner of a waste plot. Because that's what the UK is going to be soon, a waste plot."

"I thought Guernsey had enough independence," I said, still shoulder to shoulder, swaying in unison with the sergeant-major and his brother; still looking out of the car windows to see where we were heading; still hoping that, around the corner, somewhere along the string of damp deserted lanes we were using, we'd run smack into a roadblock. But the clouds were lowering and once again the fog was thickening. Outside help seemed more of a mirage than ever.

"Oh no," sighed Sir Ronald. "We had enough independence once. But we're getting sucked in. Sucked in to the center. And the center's rotten, rotten to the core. Won't hold. The Welsh know it. So do some of those Scots chaps up there. Basques, too, or so I read. But they're all stuffed with romantic silly ideas. Fourth World. Rubbish. What you need is a determined bunch of people and an island. That's what *we've* got."

"But the majority must still be against you. They aren't part of your FGM."

"Didn't your teachers teach you anything, Gull? The vanguard, that's what it's all about. Vanguard. Give the hoi polloi a lead and they'll follow. Haven't got much use for that Lenin fellow, not after living so long in that bloody country of his and yours. But he did know how to get things done, I'll say that for him."

"You also need a program," I pointed out. "Some idea of where you're leading the people *to*. Lenin wasn't just any old messiah."

"Of course. Of course," Sir Ronald snapped back.

"But I don't have to worry about that too much. I'm the military end. Leon Trotsky, eh, the prophet armed, you might say."

And the saying of it made him roar with laughter.

"Hisland's Green army," I mused. "I still don't see it doing very well against a regiment of the Greenjackets. Or even a platoon of the Queen's Own Royal Potato-Peelers."

The sergeant-major's hand tightened on the barrel of his submachine gun, but the commandant was unmoved.

"Aha! You're right, of course. Absolutely right," he went on airily. "That's where my strategy is so convincing. That's where I have it over those other fellows, those half-baked terrorists, separatists, all that mob. I've got the atomic dimension. Approved by NATO," he added with a wink.

"But when," I said, "when you've put your cat among the British pigeons, and London realizes they've got their own terrorist problem, their own separatists in the Channel Islands, with some plutonium, of course . . . what then? What are you actually going to *do?*"

"Aha! Of course you're waiting for me to tell you that, aren't you? And of course I won't do any such thing. Yet. First off, the word's got to get out. Publicity. Good thing that wretched guard on the lorry got killed. It makes them take us seriously. We—"

"And the men in the escort car. For a matter of publicity, murder's going—"

"Oh no, Gull. Don't exaggerate. Perfectly legitimate action. Retaliation. The guard killed a man of mine, don't forget, old man. Shoot and be shot, we're in the army now. But Miss Bonnissent's companions in the escort car, good heavens, no, we didn't have to kill them. Not at all. They had their hands in the air when they saw what was going on without even bothering to say Jack Robinson . . . or whatever they say in their lingo. Just tied 'em up, that's all we did. Mlle. Bonnissent'll tell you the same. This is war, Gull, Geneva Conventions."

"An advertising campaign for the Free Guernsey Movement, for Christ's sake, that's not war, or shouldn't be."

"When is a war not a war, eh? Modern dilemma. Well, let me tell you this. When it comes to the FGM, a war is a war when I say it is a war."

"Like Humpty Dumpty," I said.

It was true. I was getting a distinct feeling of being through the other side of the looking-glass, the longer I sat in the back of this Simca talking with Sir Ronald Hisland, as if I were a pawn on the chessboard of his imagination.

"Humpty Dumpty," he said in a sharp tone that brought me back to earth, "did not have enough plutonium powder to kill hundreds of thousands of people when distributed with aerosol cans in thickly populated areas."

"And is that what you plan to do?"

"You won't draw me out on that, Gull. In any case, that's not the point. It's what they'll *believe* I'm going to do."

Yes. He was right. It was pay up every time. But not just a charter of independence, surely, that wasn't the quid pro quo, was it? There was a missing link in Ronnie's plan somewhere.

I tried another tack. With no prompting, Sir Ronald was not going to bring up the subject of Mackeson-Beadle again, so I'd do it myself. "Just how long," I asked him, "do you think you can hide behind God-frey's skirts? Surely he's going to protest when he finds out you're putting the finger on him. And when he says it's all your doing, he'll have enough circumstantial evidence to prove his point, alibi or no alibi."

"Ah, so that's what you're hoping, is it?" He laughed. "Did you hear that, sa'ant-major? He's waiting for poor old Godfrey. Poor old Godot! Waiting for the old chap to up and do us down!"

"Well, where is he then?" I snapped, no longer prepared to wait patiently for answers. "And Pierre Denis? And what about the rest of them, the film crew?"

"Film crew?" Ronnie shot back. "What film crew?"

"Ah! I thought I saw a camera and lights up in Beaumont," I lied, unwilling to volunteer information. "I thought maybe you'd grabbed them too."

"Nonsense. Sergeant-major, what's he . . . ?"

"Diversion, sir. Forget it," the sergeant-major replied, breaking the silence he'd maintained during the journey so far.

"Well, the other two then?" I insisted.

But Ronnie merely asked crossly, "What's the time?"

The sergeant-major looked at his watch. "Eight-forty-ninc."

"ETA?"

"0850 at the bay. Spot on!"

"Ah! We've been chatting too much. Godfrey, eh? Ha-ha! Right, nearly there."

It didn't take me long to realize that "there" meant a spot on the coastline only a kilometer from Diélette and the *auberge,* a place not altogether unfamiliar. For our destination was that same abandoned iron mine Pierre had pointed out to me on the Cap de Flamanville.

Chapter 5

December 15.   8:52 A.M.

AS WE piled out I looked up and around. It was an impressively miserable place, a tomb to generations of overworked and underpaid miners, gaunt, rotting, yet bleakly defying its abandonment to time and sea fogs. Above, disappearing into the cloud, was the white tower. The tall structure was quite new, made of white-washed concrete. Its white surface, however, only served to emphasize the grimness of the ancient black-ened granite all around.

Looking up at the tower I could see the lower part of the square overhang that sat like a huge doll's house on top of the bare concrete support. Threatening, as it were, from across the way was an array of great dark granite silos, or accumulators, which stood braced against the side of the cliff, supported by a line of flying buttresses like the walls of Winchester Cathedral. On one of the buttresses a handrail ran up its outer curve, turning the serrated blocks of granite into a makeshift staircase. Rectangular holes at the bottom of the silos were all that remained of a system of sluice-gates that once controlled the flood of accumulated ore, releasing it and sending it tumbling down on the first stage of its journey out to boats waiting at the end of the line of iron pylons.

All around, a debris of spattered iron-ore chips and coal dust was turning to smears of slurry in the drenching fog.

Twenty yards away at the base of the left-hand silo, between a pile of iron ore and the first of the flying buttresses, the Renault van was already parked.

I had time to notice only one other thing—a kind of painted scroll on the wall of the white tower which read *"N.-D. du Bon Secours"* on top and *"Priez pour nous"* below—before I felt the prod of the submachine gun in my backbone.

Somehow this appeal to Our Lady With the Helping Hand seemed more threatening than reassuring. I've never felt comfortable having to rely on intercession from on high.

The doorway directly in front of us was bricked in, and we were goaded around the side of the tower. Inside, a faint light shone. I turned to enter a gap in the wall from which a screen of crisscrossed barbed wire had been pulled aside, but the man with the gun barked instead, "Straight on, Russkoff! Get in that shed there!"

I walked another five yards, my feet squelching, Sophie Bonnissent at my elbow. We ducked under a rusty iron rope and threaded our way through a jumble of flaky henna-colored wheels and cables. On our right was a keyhole-shaped structure that looked as if it were the top of one of the mineshafts. Its corrugated asbestos roof was as ragged as Cinderella's pre-party dress. Beside it was a brick shed, relatively intact except for a rotting wooden door that stood wide open.

"Halt!"

I halted. The girl stumbled, clutched at my arm, held on.

"Watch 'em, Number Five."

"Sir!"

A man I hadn't seen before stepped out of the shed, grinning, revealing black stubs where teeth had been.

"Hold it there, boyos!"

The Welsh voice was new to me too. Its mean-looking owner was six inches below my six feet, grizzled and streaked with dirty rain. Like the sergeant-major, he too had a gun.

What was almost a ray of sunlight flickered, then dimmed. My eye caught the Renault van again, over to my left. Inside it I could just make out the bars of the cages, shining like huge silvery glow-worms. Then a puff of wet dawn fog drifted in off the sea and passed directly between me and the van. Others, larger and thicker, followed, at first in separate waves, then in a rush of wider, higher rollers. It became impossible to see what was going on. For me . . . and for anyone who might happen to pass. Nature was conspiring with Ronnie to keep his operations secret.

Yet the shed was only twenty yards or so from the van. I stood just inside to keep dry but still observe what was happening. Sophie Bonnissent held onto my arm.

She gripped me with tight but not, I felt, nervous fingers. The Welsh guard saw us and gestured with his gun for us to get completely back inside. I played dumb and stayed where I was. Fortunately Sir Ronald came striding up at that moment.

"Right, young lady," he boomed. "Let's have 'em open. Can't hang around all day. Miss Bonnissent!"

Her fingers dug in tighter. She stared at him blankly.

"Oh God," he muttered, then called out, "Hurry up, Gull. Bring her over. Make yourself useful while you're still . . ."

A drip of foggy drizzle formed on the tip of my nose. I brushed it off with the back of my hand. As we walked toward the van, I turned to Sophie and said in French, "The old fool wants us to show him how to open his Christmas present."

The sergeant-major, who had just come into earshot, glared at me. Then he climbed up inside the back of the van, squeezing in beside the four containers.

"Of course I can't open them," Sophie said firmly. "They are securely locked, as you can see. For obvious reasons they don't carry keys on the transports. I could have told him that before if he'd asked."

I translated.

"Good God, I know there're no bloody *keys,*" Sir Ronald roared. "I just want her to stand by and tell me if there's any danger of the things going bang while we get on with the job."

At that moment the sergeant-major's brother came out of the mist at a fast trot, wheeling a cart with a bottle of compressed gas and an oxyacetylene torch. A pair of protective goggles was pushed up on his forehead.

"Don't imagine she won't speak up if we do something rash," said Sir Ronald with quiet sarcasm.

The torch flared.

The tip of the flame focused into a sharp point and bit into the ring of the padlock that sealed the first of the steel casings. Sophie flinched but said nothing. The sergeant-major himself, from his inside perch, waited until the ring was red hot, then produced a small crowbar, inserted it and twisted until the ring snapped.

"Aren't you going to tell them it's dangerous, too much heat?" I said to Sophie out of the side of my mouth, knowing that the soft sounds wouldn't carry too far in competition with the roar of the blowtorch.

She shook her head. "He knows it's not," she whispered back. "I don't want to try any tricks yet."

"I had started to tell him he wouldn't find any plutonium inside. Dummy load. Worth trying?"

Sophie considered, watching the flame all the while. "I'll see."

Then we stood in silence.

She was amazingly calm, despite all she'd been through. Pale-faced, wet and dirty, she could still seem to be on top of the situation, still retain her cool control. I guessed she was about thirty, a good age . . . I forced myself to look at the flame.

The man with the blowtorch seemed to be aware that he shouldn't point it directly at the flask containing the plutonium, but Sophie never took her eyes off what he was doing.

The flame dipped and dived like a woodpecker's beak rapping at the steel, dancing away when too close to the deadly plutonium, returning to peck as close as it dared. Sweat beaded on the brother's face around the rim of his goggles. I felt I was in a dentist's chair, the drill zinging in and out of a cavity, waiting, wincing, panicked by the

idea that a millimeter away was the naked nerve. Another siren wailed . . . in the distance. It wasn't the
moment to put the dentist into a panic. Let them shut
up out there till he'd done!

My glance flicked away again and up toward a piece
of cliff that I could glimpse through the fog over to my
right. Maybe some hardy walker would happen along,
some shepherd with his dog? But no one was up there
on that fragment of cliff, not even a roving sheep or
goat. Besides, the wet blanket of fog that flapped around
us hid us effectively from any passer-by. Already the
one lucky break in the mist had closed up.

Inside the van, however, things weren't going altogether Ronnie's way, after all . . . .

A problem had arisen: how to safely extract the
plutonium bottles from the protective cylinders now
that the locks had all been burnt through.

The sergeant-major fumbled inside one of them, then
winced as he felt the heat given off by the radioactive
substance. Sophie was about to say something, but
stopped as soon as he removed his hand. The whole
operation was beginning to seem to me foolhardy, if not
plain crazy. I'd never imagined you could come so close
to plutonium. Just how much could you get away with?
Didn't those bottles emit neutrons? Or something? I
suspected only Sophie Bonnissent really knew just what
the dangers were.

The sergeant-major made another attempt to lift out
a canister.

"*Merde!*" he exclaimed and carried on swearing like
a carter.

I grinned at Sophie and began humming to myself the
tune of a Russian song. I alone knew that the words
were about dawn breaking and a bright light flooding

over the fields and farms; in the second verse, I adapted the words that babbled of fields and farms to the Russian for cliffs and mines.

The sergeant-major hissed at me to shut up. It was almost full daylight now. Maybe the sun, rising up there somewhere, would generate enough heat to disperse the mist? If so, had Sir Ronald posted other men to head off the curious? Not many. The troops at the mine were no longer at full strength: just the sergeant-major, brother Georges, the two others who had driven the Simca and the Renault van, and the Welshman. Of the absent, one had been deployed to dump the plutonium truck like a false clue in a treasure hunt, and the redhead had pedaled off to oblivion. One was dead.

As for the driver of the Renault, the only one remaining whom I hadn't already identified by sight, he turned out to be a short, middle-aged man with Celtic, or maritime, or mildly alcoholic, coloring; he came up now behind the van, cradling a gun. By a process of elimination, he had to be the one with the deep voice, the very first voice I'd heard when I woke up en route to the hijacking.

The other man, the Simca's driver for the return trip, disappeared up the cliff path to my right, long hair flapping in the wind, perhaps to act as lookout.

Sir Ronald came up beside me.

"Why don't you keep it in the containers and have done with it?" I said.

He looked at me and nodded. "Not trying to pretend it's coal dust in there any more, eh, Gull?"

"I didn't say it was coal dust. Still, if you . . ." I tried to find something convincing to say but Sir Ronald Hisland interrupted.

"No, no, old boy. I want the stuff out of there. Plans

are plans, and we must stick to them."

"What plans?"

"Decoy. Actually, since you ask, I'm going to leave the stuff, I mean the cages, empty of course, on board poor old Godfrey's boat." He guffawed.

"His boat? Isn't he . . . ? Didn't he sail away in it?"

"Sailed away for a year and a day to the land where the Bong-tree grows," said Sir Ronald, and laughed again loudly. "Poor old Godfrey. But he had to do it."

I didn't get it. If Ronnie had Mackeson-Beadle's boat . . . ?

"Merde!"

The sergeant-major's curse interrupted my thoughts as again he repeated his impression of picking a hot potato out of a saucepan. But this time he'd mastered the trick of snatching it out before it burned him.

I watched fascinated as he did the same thing three more times, wearing only a thin pair of leather gloves. It still seemed incredibly foolhardy to me. But he acted as if he knew what he was doing. I looked at Sophie. If she was worried, she didn't betray it. In a matter of seconds the sergeant-major had grabbed the four cans out of the cylinders, one after the other, and placed them about a yard apart along the bottom of the silo.

Then Sophie moved onstage.

"Mais . . . this material," she said, peering at the first bottle to be extracted from its container, then at the other three in turn, "it is not plutonium! Well, at least it is plutonium, but it's not in dioxide powder form. It's the manganese-coated pellets. Vitrified manganese. You would need a million-dollar installation to get the coating off and make it dangerous." She broke out into a strained laugh.

I didn't bother to translate. Let it sink in slowly.

The brother, about to pick up the nearest bottle and put it on his trolley, stopped in mid-gesture, as if a film projector had jammed.

Nobody spoke.

Was it a bluff? Delaying tactics? My idea being used?

Sir Ronald made the first move—a deeply puzzled creasing of his forehead. "What . . . ? Magnesium, did she say?"

The sergeant-major grasped the implications more clearly and quickly. He thought hard for a second. Then without waiting for me to translate the original message to Sir Ronald into English, he burst out himself, "She means it's not in regular powder form. It's in pellets with a protective layer of a hard metal around each pellet, and we can't get through. I've heard about that system. But I don't believe a fucking word."

"Eh? What's it say on these things here?" Sir Ronald snapped.

But one thing was sure: none of us except Sophie could make head or tail of the hieroglyphs stenciled all over the two-liter tin cans. I recognized the plutonium dioxide symbol—PuO_2—and the weight, given as "3,400 grammes." That was all. Everyone's eyes were doing the same as mine, ranging along the lines of figures and symbols as if each can was a Rosetta stone holding the secret to the ancient Egyptian script.

There was again a moment before anyone spoke.

Then Sir Ronald said, "Coating?" rather feebly, and tried to make up for it with a resolute stare at Sophie.

"It's a protective measure we've just introduced. A film of manganese. Thin but hard, solid and metallurgically bonded, over each pellet. Only one in twenty shipments is even scheduled to be in this form and only a quarter of each load. You've just struck it unlucky. If you want the regular dioxide powder, you'll have to fetch the truck back."

This time I translated.

"It's harmless, you mean? Quite harmless?" he shot back.

"Unless you can find a way to heat the pellets—*pastilles,* we call them—to a thousand degrees and a bit more. Centigrade."

"If the bitch knew . . ." I heard the sergeant-major begin.

"The best-laid schemes o' mice an' men . . ." I interrupted loudly, cheerfully.

Everybody just stood there, waiting for Sir Ronald's decision. The sergeant-major's expression flickered between incredulity and anger. Sophie's expression didn't change. I was beginning to wonder myself. She was convincing. And did I merely imagine, too, a ray of sunlight dipping through a slit in the gray fog? Probably. There was no relief to the gloom when I looked up and studied the sky directly.

Again, the wail of a police car! Nearer.

As if prompted by the danger signal, the disconcerted commandant said quickly, "Then why's the stuff in these damn containers if it's no danger? Eh?"

"Because there is a slight risk in the long term of radioactive contamination," Sophie said quickly but with calm assurance. "But mainly because no one has yet got around to designing special equipment for transporting this treated material. It's too new. But we will, do not worry."

Sir Ronald grunted. He knew enough about bureaucracies to sense that the explanation was perfectly plausible.

I smiled at Sophie, and she smiled back, a warm conspiratorial smile.

If it was a bluff, it was working remarkably well. On the other hand, as far as I knew, it might be true. Why not? And if it were true, and the police knew about it, which they would by now, so much for Sir Ronald Hisland's blackmail threats!

The commandant was red-faced. He looked at his watch, frowned. "How hot's that blowtorch get, sergeant-major?" he asked suddenly.

It was the brother who answered. "Six hundred degrees, sir."

"Centigrade?"

The brother nodded.

"Well, then, that's all right. Won't hurt at all. Those lozenge things are safe up to a thousand, you say? Mademoiselle, come here. Yes. Right here, by this bottle thing, this can. Carry on, working party. Get the fire going and open the bloody thing up. We'll see, by God, if it's safe."

Of course it was not. Not safe at all.

Sophie put a stop to the operation before the blowtorch was even lit.

"Sorry," she sighed to me. "Just a coincidence, but regular plutonium dioxide, which this really is, happens to react strongly to a temperature of six hundred degrees. That would have been . . . unpleasant for all of us."

"No manganese then?" I said with a sigh. "No coating?"

Sophie sighed, too, saying no more. Our eyes met. We smiled again—though weakly. It had been worth a try.

The bluff exposed, the cylinders were immediately manhandled one by one on the gasburner's trolley into the base of the tall white tower.

We all followed. The interior of the tower which I now viewed for the first time was a vast echoing space, one of the grimmest, ugliest, dampest places I had ever seen. Skeletons of the winches that had once hauled ore from the seams lay rotting against the wall, silent and sinister as the grave. The main hall was an iron-age tomb where the bones of some fabled giant, mutilated by enemies and mangled by time and by the sinking of the tomb walls, had been miraculously, haphazardly preserved in the form of sawed-off concrete pillars and rusty stanchions, with smaller bones and flakes of skin transformed into worm-eaten planks and chips of ore.

An icy wind reinforced the necropolitan gloom.

I looked up overhead, but a concrete ceiling a third of the way up the tower blocked the view. Down at my feet a stairway appeared to lead to a lower floor but stopped at a concrete wall, solid except for a low rusty iron door padlocked shut. All around there were chalked on the damp surfaces revolutionary slogans from 1968, mostly crossed out or superimposed by counter-slogans. *"À bas les étudiants!"* and *"Tout pouvoir à de Gaulle!"* outnumbered such graffiti as *"Merde aux bourgeois!"* and *"US=SS."*

A wisp of fog entered behind us like a specter. My body shivered despite my efforts at self-control. Then Sir Ronald beckoned and made me stand in front of him like a schoolboy before the headmaster. A fleeting—and welcome—anger provided me a hint of warmth.

"Fascinating, eh? Little wagon things brought the stuff up to here from a hundred and fifty yards down under. Seams went right out under the sea. Good, enough guided tour. Stay there, Gull. Carry on, sa'ant-major."

The sergeant-major was eager for action.

"*Allez,* mademoiselle, let's make this stuff safe. Russko, you help her."

Sophie shook her head, immobile just inside the door. "You have to handle plutonium with great caution. Unless you are properly shielded, it's suicide to do more than you have already done, to touch the canisters even briefly. For contact longer than a few seconds you need extensive protection against neutron bombardment."

Sir Ronald enjoyed that idea.

"What better protection than you, my dear. As long as *you're* along the job'll be properly done. My trump card. Ace of trumps. Otherwise we all get frazzled together."

I translated for Sophie while his laugh echoed around the burial chamber. As it died away, I became conscious of the noise of the sea breaking against the rocks below like coal being dropped into a ship's hold. It sounded like millions of bottles being crunched and squeezed in a giant press.

I edged toward the outer wall.

Sir Ronald noticed but didn't try to stop me. "No escape that way, but don't go too far," he said. "Not that I should care if you fell out, but there's a kind of chute thing that's never been bricked up."

I peered down cautiously at an enormous rusty structure that pierced the north wall of the tower overlooking the sea. At least six feet wide, the chute extended out into space at a dipping forty-five-degree angle. Way, way below, the sea churned around the top of a glistening rock, swirling then sucking backward before exploding, time and again, in a brutal insistent attempt to pound the granite into sand. Even in the dim light, I could see the spray flying.

The wind gave a wolf-howl in the top of the tower and a curl of fog danced on the lip of the chute, before the wind snapped it away again.

"Now then!" Ronnie called. I took a couple of paces back. Miss Bonnissent was brought forward and asked to point out the best places to store the plutonium.

I translated again, listened to her reply, then let her indicate a row of niches where the concrete protection was adequate for the job.

One of the plutonium canisters was still on the trolley, so I tipped it off into the first of the hiding places, behind a pillar with the simplest message chalked on it —*"Con!"* I felt like an idiot too. Brother Georges, in the interest of speed, loaded the other three with his gloved hands. Very quickly all the cylinders were out of sight.

"There we are. Easy. Could have done it with your fingers in your nose, right, that what you say, sergeant-major? Ha!" The man in question scowled, but Ronnie Hisland carried on regardless. "Now it's just a matter of time and tide. Unfortunately, neither of 'em hurries for any man. That's all for now. You two hang on in the shed until we're ready to move. No tricks, Gull. Don't want to lose your privileges, eh?"

"Privileges?"

"You're alive, aren't you? Now get out! Sa'ant-major, keep Number Five on guard."

The sergeant-major turned Sophie and me around with the muzzle of his gun.

"Mon Dieu," she said as we stumbled past the old pithead and into the shed, damp, brick-lined, smelling of stale cigarettes and lit by a small grimy skylight. "My

God, I see what you mean, Vladimir, he's *really* got spiders in his ceiling!"

IT WAS so dark in that shed that it took me some time to make out the food, drink and magazines stacked in the corner behind the door—scotch, beer, an array of tins, Mother's Pride bread, French and English cigarettes, old copies of *Paris-Match* and *Charlie-Hebdo*. Enough for a siege. Slowly my eyes moved around the ten-foot-long walls. Neither of us realized that someone else was already inside until he spoke. The voice was familiar yet distorted, as if by pain. I couldn't be sure who it was until the feeble light glinted on square-framed glasses.

"Pierre!"

Pierre Denis gave another grunt. I knelt down beside him quickly, Sophie on his other side. She found my hand across his body and held on tight, though she didn't seem the fainting type. Pierre had been beaten. The blood was mostly cleaned off, judging by the smears on his cheeks and chin, but his lips were torn. I made out bruise marks around his eyes.

Sophie withdrew her hand from mine and put a finger and thumb on the young man's pulse. The pressure on his wrist seemed to revive him.

"Bastards," he muttered. "They made me. They knew it all already but they made me tell them. I thought I could . . . ." He began to sob.

"Rest," Sophie said softly. "I can see you were too brave."

"Did they . . . did they do it?"

I nodded. "Yes."

He looked into our eyes, from me to Sophie and back.

127

I realized he didn't know who she was. I told him. I was about to explain things in reverse to Sophie but she cut me short.

"I recognize you," she said to Pierre. "I have often seen your picture in the *Presse de la Manche.*"

He smiled, then shuddered. "What is the time?"

"Quarter after nine," I said.

"Then the *flics* will be here soon," he said, with sudden confidence. "So long as the fog has cleared, the helicopters . . ."

"It hasn't," I said.

"Have they still got the . . . powder? Here?"

"In the tower, yes."

"Is the boat in?"

"Boat?"

"They are docking the boat in Diélette so as to ship out the plutonium. The tide will be high enough at eleven. I heard them say so. They are storing it here until ten minutes before the tide crests, then taking it to the port. It is too dangerous to load from these cliffs."

"So there's still ninety minutes or so for the police to find this place before we move," I said with a surge of new hope.

"But the fog," Pierre muttered. "They'll never . . . I told them the route. I couldn't help it, they said it was only to confirm, but I . . . ."

He shook his head violently and pushed himself up onto his knees, then his feet. He staggered a little, but kept upright. "I must see if it is clearing," he said, more resolutely than I'd have believed possible. But there was something manic in his voice that disturbed me.

He opened the door, which was so slimy with moss and so warped that it couldn't be locked, and looked out. Could they possibly have forgotten to post a guard?

"Shut that fucking door, boyo, or I'll blow your balls off!"

They hadn't forgotten.

Pierre pulled himself back in and stood propped against the wall beside the door.

Ten seconds passed like an hour.

Pierre reminded me suddenly of a young man my unit took for questioning in Budapest, on the very first day of the riots back in October 1956. A Hungarian student tried to harangue some of us Red army soldiers when we first arrived in his capital city, running alongside our tanks. When he got no response, though he was persuasive and had a good knowledge of Russian, he began organizing a crowd to resist. My commanding officer ordered him seized and taken along for "questioning." I was detailed to show him out again after his ordeal. He was transformed, hangdog, with a bitter look in his eyes. The mere sight of his interrogators had unnerved him. He had begun to confess to all kinds of political peccadilloes, like a guilt-ridden adolescent at his first confession, even before anyone had time to put a question. In fact—and this was at the very beginning of our intervention when we still thought we were there to help, not to bully—his captors' intention had been only to persuade the young Hungarian of the Red Army's benevolence. Certainly my commanding officer was a decent man, a Finn by origin. He might have gotten on well with someone whose native language was so nearly comprehensible.

But fear was the only emotion the young man felt, a shaming, dominating fear.

I wondered what happened to him after his release? Did he rush to the barricades to revenge his humiliation? Did he lock himself up till the troubles were over, keep his head down and join the winning side when he knew which it was?

Yet although Pierre looked like that young man, his case was different. By resisting at all, he had been, as Sophie said, too brave. He probably wasn't even a hero by nature, which made his resistance all the more admirable.

"I must . . . I must get a . . . ."

Pierre was talking more to himself than to us. He opened the door again, before I could stop him.

"I said shut that fucking . . ."

It slammed shut. But Pierre stayed on the other side of it. I made a move to follow. Sophie held me back. Voices were heard outside, then a pause.

I pulled myself out of Sophie's grip and pulled at the protesting door. A buffet of wet air slapped my face. The door itself fell off its rusty hinges and clattered to the ground.

It saved Pierre's life. The guard, two hands wielding his submachine gun, was poised to swing the stock around into the young man's face. Suddenly he was caught in two minds—to immobilize Pierre . . . or aim a bullet at me. In the split-second delay Pierre had his hand on a large chunk of iron ore. The Welshman saw what was happening and began to swivel back around, but Pierre ducked under the gun-butt and with a windmilling right hook thumped fist and rock into the guard's right temple. He staggered, stunned. I met his falling body with the toe of my right shoe. The first kick sank into his stomach. He flipped over, and the next caught him on the bridge of his nose. He collapsed, bleeding messily from the nose and the side of his head. I wanted the gun, but the guard had fallen on top of it. Its barrel stuck out tantalizingly. I knelt and tugged at it to get it free. The Welshman rolled off and I grabbed it triumphantly.

"Freeze!"

The sergeant-major's shouted order had an instant effect. My body froze. I might have been an ice-carving. Only my lips moved as I swore.

"Okay. Move!" he yelled. "Get back!"

Slowly I unfroze, retreated about five yards and stopped. He jerked his gun and I backed off two more paces. It wasn't much, but I hoped I was providing something of a distraction. Then, inadvertently, I looked around for Pierre. He had gone. I knew it didn't matter where, but my curiosity got the better of me. It alerted the sergeant-major. He too began searching around with wild, darting eyes. Seconds later his gaze became fixed. I cursed and followed his line of sight toward the staircase that climbed precipitously up the side of the granite bunker. At the very top was a small, struggling, still rising figure.

Standing astride the spread-eagled body of the Welshman, the sergeant-major fixed Pierre Denis with his eyes like a hunter.

"Hold it," he yelled. Then, *"Arrête-toi!"*

Pierre kept climbing.

Another figure came out of the fog to my right at a fast shuffle. Face purple, eyes staring, panting up behind the sergeant-major, Ronnie Hisland croaked an order. "Get him!"

It was superfluous. The sergeant-major had already acted.

Too far away to do anything, I watched appalled as he raised his gun to his shoulder, flicked a small lever, aimed carefully and . . . fired.

A single shot, a well-trained rhythm. Much too quick

for me to cover the distance between us.

Pierre was just going over the top, clutching at the wall, holding on, beginning to crawl. Another yard and he'd have been across the wall and swallowed up by the dark and the mist and the distance.

The single shot stopped him . . . dead.

But he didn't fall. Not at once. His fingers kept their grip on the rough granite, like grappling hooks. Only when his legs, then his whole body, began to slip sideways over the far edge of the wall did the strain, little by little, become too great. Finally his grip snapped loose.

Against a backdrop of the seething clouds and the eerie shapes of the mine buildings, the whole action had something of the staged about it. The horror it inspired parodied the classical rules. Then something happened that Greek drama would never have allowed, something blackly . . . comic almost, which brought home the real horror.

Through one of the rectangular holes at the base of the bunker a body suddenly dropped, slid forward onto the brim, then fell out, splaying over a pile of ore and discarded junk like a bent nickel in a coin return.

There was a moment when everyone stared at this thing that had popped out of the hole in the dark of the December dawn. I stared, too; it was the first time I'd seen a person killed in cold blood. In the heat of war, of passion, yes, I had witnessed that, but never a man picked off this way, like a pheasant trapped in a hedge, like a plastic duck at a fairground. I felt nauseated; my knees began to buckle. I had to lock them stiff.

Then, as on my last day in Hungary in 1956, my numbness abruptly left me and I felt the urge to *run*.

I turned and caught Sophie's eye. The contact jerked her out of her own gaping shock.

Then she pointed. The sergeant-major, Sir Ronald and the deep-voiced Celt were all three over by the base of the silo where Pierre's body had tumbled out. How long did we have before they remembered to attend to us? There was no time to reflect. A low wall to our right gave us cover. We both ran, ducking low. I know I slammed into a block of cement spiked with twisted iron bars, but felt nothing. The shambles of the old pithead was a maze, but it afforded thicker and thicker cover. What we needed, though, was the cliff . . . and the enveloping mist. Sophie tugged my sleeve and pointed again. She began breathing hard.

"This way." She ran out through a roofless passage that had once been a long narrow shed.

A muffled cry came from my left. Another.

Glancing over my shoulder, I could see nobody.

"Quick!" Sophie hissed.

We kept running. Fast. Away—anywhere. Suddenly a wall confronted us. But a natural wall of granite and tufts of damp grass. We were beyond the giant silos. Freedom!

WHAT HAPPENED between 0919 (the figure I saw on my watch as I clutched the cliff face two hundred yards from the mine and fifty above it) and 1013 when the watch stopped for good is still unclear. But I'll try to reconstruct.

Two memories are overwhelming . . . that Sophie Bonnissent was with me, close to me, all that time. And the fog.

The fog was our ally . . . at first. We had only twenty

seconds' start, yet although the shouting below and to our left meant they knew we'd gone, they couldn't know precisely where. Even more important, the cliff itself was invisible six feet above or below. It was only the lack of a view that kept my nerves intact.

Shots were fired, shots or curses or the slamming of car doors, only God is sure. But we had plunged into another world, as remote from Ronnie and the sergeant-major as from civilization . . . or, as yet, from help.

The top of the cliff arrived abruptly and definitively; no further crests, just thickets of wet, spiny gorse and open patches of grass slippery with goat and sheep droppings. Sophie, scrabbling like a crab, pulled herself the final vertical yard and joined me. We hurled ourselves together into the gorse, reached an impasse and stopped.

Streams of vapor from our panting mouths shot extra steam into the already mist-drenched atmosphere.

"Do you know these cliffs, the cape up here?" I gasped as Sophie clutched at me, holding me back from beginning the mad rush again so soon.

"No. No, but it . . . it shouldn't be hard if we keep in a . . . a straight line. How long have we got until they move?"

"An hour and a half, maybe more. Eleven is the earliest the tide can get them out of the harbor."

"That is good," she said, her words coming smoother. "Flamanville, the village, can't be far. There must be a telephone, a gendarme, something there."

"Onward and upward. Except first it has to be backward. Want to play leader?"

"Save your feminism, Vladimir," she shot back with the first trace of a smile. "Be an old-time hunter!"

I hesitated another moment, realizing we'd already

made some twists and turns since the cliff top. There was no sound out of the fog, no lighter patches hinting at the sun behind. A compass would have helped.

Sophie said impatiently, *"Allez!"*

I set off more in hope than certainty, influenced by the gaps in the gorse rather than a hunter's intuition, of which I had none. She followed. Two buttons had been ripped off her suede coat. In the fissure between her lapels, the bodies of cashmere butterflies palpitated. I felt an untimely urge to throw her down into the dirt at our feet and make animal love. What was she doing appealing to primitive instincts? Didn't she know where *they* led?

A goat path crossed my own track at right angles, and I took the same path, going right without hesitation. In a couple of yards it led to ruined walls, the remains of a small granite hut, a goatherd's maybe, or the abandoned shelter of a customs patrol. Then it petered out.

"Merde!"

I wished I were a better soldier. Hadn't cross-country treks without a map, night marches, initiative tests all been part of my Red army training? Amanda's first husband was a soldier; a major, and heading for promotion. Would that bastard've done better than me? Why do I have such a phobia about the military? Hell, I like disliking them.

No, I told myself, pushing on through the prickly gorse, the Red army isn't, or wasn't, worse than any other army. It just happened to be the army I . . . deserted from. I even admire the Red army, from a safe distance. Good God, I was supposed to have imbibed the valor of Marshal Zhukov, not to mention the will of Generalissimo Stalin, like milk from the great Soviet

135

breast of Mother Russia. I was fed on the exploits of Civil and Great Patriotic Wars as young Americans are fed Valley Forge and Iwo Jima, as English children learn to rally behind the Redcoats, the Light Brigade and the Desert Rats. Yet I cling to attitudes that would make Vladimir Ilyich turn over in his mausoleum and my Marxism-Leninism teacher go red with shame. I mean, I don't like killing of any sort, not even of the class enemy. I know why. I'm a member of the bourgeoisie now.

And now where was I? *Gospodi!* My mind had gone blank. What had I been thinking about? My thoughts faded like a dream on waking. The hell with that—where *were* we?

Where too was Sophie? Was it safe to shout? Had I been going too fast? She came scrambling out of the dripping gorse and the fog just as I was working up to a panic.

"Not so . . . not so . . ." The butterflies were going berserk as her breasts heaved with the effort to catch her breath.

"Fast," I supplied, gasping myself. "Sorry."

She smiled. God! That smile again. What blue, blue eyes. Ultramarine. What a contrast to Amanda she was, what a contrast to that dun-eyed, bay-haired, large-boned public-school Madonna. How had I gotten into . . . ? I knew. It was *her* fault, wasn't it? Don't go over it again, I told myself. Not now. Concentrate on getting out of this freezing wasteland, this nature's mirror maze stuck on a man-forsaken headland at the end of France.

"Here are the mists," I challenged the fog, in a sudden anti-Keatsian burst, "but where the hell's the mellow fruitfulness?"

"Blasphemy. You should know better," said Sophie

136

. . . in perfect, delicately accented *English*.

"So you . . . !"

"But why should I tell Mr. Hisland?"

She was not dumb either.

"*Sir* Ronald," I muttered sharply. "If the bloody Queen had only had sense enough to bring the sword down with a bit more of a flourish! Okay again? Let's go."

"You know, Vladimir," she said behind me as we scrambled over and around more rocks, more gorse bushes, more boggy holes, "I never have found out what all this is about."

I suddenly realized. How could she know? So, still on the march, I gave her a rundown.

"You don't believe all that, do you?" she said at the end, back into French. "Stop. I must rest for ten seconds." Hair was straggling in wet tangles over her face, but she let it stay there. "Free Guernsey? It's madness. It can't be real."

"He killed Pierre Denis. Had him killed. You saw that. He also killed a guard at the hijack. Isn't that enough to convince you?"

"That he's crazy, yes. That he has some plan, some vision maybe. But to convince me that he can use plutonium for those purposes, this is impossible."

It seemed as crazy to me as it did to her. "Tell me quickly one thing about plutonium," I said, "then let's get on. It's . . . it's already after half past nine. What can he do with it, right now? Is it dangerous there at the mine? What are the chances of his contaminating himself first?"

"It's a question of handling," Sophie said, speaking quickly. "Of course if the canister's pierced and you inhale the powder, that's it. But even the intact canisters mustn't come too close to the body. Nor must two of them be brought close to each other. In the first case, the body will act as a kind of reactant, a 'moderator.' It will activate excessively the particles, which will then bombard and cause fatal cell damage in the body. In the second case, if the canisters touch, we risk reaching a critical mass as well as activating the particles."

"Critical? You mean it explodes?"

"Not necessarily. But it reacts, and there is a lot of dangerous heat and radiation."

"Umm."

"And what are these particles?"

"Neutrons. Electrons. Gamma rays. Lots and lots of alpha particles that are pretty harmless. Otherwise a variety of *petits monstres.*"

"But keep it all away from everybody and from itself and it's okay?"

"It should be."

"Umm. I still don't get it."

"Look, Vladimir, this isn't the moment for a lecture in nuclear physics. Just believe me when I say if you go too close to the things they get very nasty. Don't ever get sentimental about one of those canisters and give it a hug. The water of which your body is largely composed slows the neutrons down and makes you quite sick. Dead, eventually. All right?"

I wanted to object that my body wasn't made up exclusively of water. I could prove it. Instead I said, "If water does that, I suppose it'd be even worse if you took a canister out in the rain? Or into the bath with you?"

Sophie laughed—but quickly. "It would. Look, for God's sake let's get going. Actually what you said reminds me. I'll tell you a story—on the run."

"*Allons-y!*"

138

We pushed on, not exactly running but walking fast.

"It happened in the States, Colorado maybe, I forget," Sophie said, speaking to the back of my head. "Some plutonium contaminated a cooling bath by mistake. There was already some other radioactive material in there. The reaction was set up. The technician standing nearby was thrown to the ground. Believe it or not, and this was an expert, a trained technician, he got up and resumed his work, and then it really hit him. His whole body felt it was burning. Nothing was visible except a blue flash as the reaction started. Mad with pain, he threw himself through a plate-glass window because he could see snow on the ground outside. He had to reach it, throw himself into it to drive away the heat. He was crazed by the radiation burns he had sustained and he rolled over and over in the snow as if he were on fire."

"Did he put it out?"

"An hour later he was dead. That kind of burning cannot be extinguished."

After that, we walked in silence for a minute.

Sophie broke the spell. "Vladimir, where the hell are we going?"

I stopped. So suddenly that she ran into me.

"You guessed!" I said. "I know. I'm lost. Totally at sea. If you think you're a better guide, sweetheart . . . ."

"No. But we *must* find a house, a telephone—soon. Shall we shout?"

Shout at the wind! I laughed. She gave a Gallic shrug, one of those *beaux gestes* that tell you all you need to know. Then she flung her arms around my neck, half-opened her mouth and kissed me . . . a kiss that ran through my body and made me think again about radiation. As abruptly, she let me go.

"That was to change the . . . bad vibrations," she whispered. I was trembling like a teenager.

We ran forward again. Yes, we were at sea up here. That's how it felt to me, anyway—drowning in the fog in the middle of the ocean, as if the collision with the film crew were a mere rehearsal . . . as if everything since had been a drowning man's nightmare. So far I had been struggling to keep myself afloat, treading water among the gorse and heaps of rock. But now suddenly I went under. Literally . . . I stumbled into a freshwater spring.

Before Sophie came to pull me out, my life began to flash before me, just as they say it does. Moscow, slushy streets in wartime, my pinch-faced mother smelling of cabbage soup boiled from snow, always at the stove in our one-room apartment by the new Ring Road, her stomach rumbling but she eating nothing—not even to taste—before I had my fill; pioneer meetings, frozen nostrils, the funeral of a school friend who committed suicide, not really a funeral, a gathering at his house, everyone crying. And the good things, later . . . my English teacher, Pavel Nicolaevich Ivanov, former OGPU undercover agent in London who loved the English; Kaganopuss, my cat; my first girl . . . .

I was free, my whole body wet. My Frye boots weighed ten kilos, and I was still stretched out flat. But I was on the surface again.

Exhaustion and frustration were smeared on Sophie's face, too, along with the mud and the mascara and the rain.

"Vladimir, you must watch where you are stepping. Come on. We should have found a house a long time ago. This is not the Camargue."

"We're going in circles. It's a whirlpool and we're being sucked into the center."

She seized my arm and pulled me to my feet. I kissed her hand in the Russian style.

"Vladimir! *Mon Dieu!*"

"Divine as always."

"You're going soft. Head *and* body."

"I know. You lead."

She did, and as we floundered on, my mind went under again . . . .

A holiday in Sukhumi, fat white bodies on the Black Sea beach . . . Matushka Volga and the pungent smell of *ukha,* the muddy bouillabaisse I remember eating on her banks . . . school outings and hydrofoils on crazy patterns of rivers and lakes, and Nina Petrovna Lushnikova, who showed me her breasts but told me I was too young to touch . . . .

I fell, got up, kept walking.

A student at Moscow University, skating in Gorki Park with Natasha, the silver-blue cupolas of Novgorod one Sunday in spring, Soviet army barracks where the last shred of privacy vanished, buttoned up in high-collared uniforms, Boris Yakovlevich's vodka-still that he made from a czarist samovar, smashed by a vigilante, a *druzhinik* . . . Boris was a Jew. Budapest, that noisy tank . . . a long journey to the West . . . .

It was strange. After that, no memories. The newsreel stopped in 1956. Figures flashed through my brain like the countdown at the end of a reel. Had my lungs filled with fog, had I stopped breathing? A hand shook me.

"Vladimir! You're bleeding, your head!"

I put my hand to my left ear and it came away red-brown. The blackjack wound had reopened, was throbbing now. We were in a valley, following a stream. I bent down and daubed clean ice-cold water on my temples, then dragged myself on.

"It's no use," I heard myself say. "There's no one left alive."

"Vladimir!"

"Like pissing into a violin, the sergeant-major would say."

Her sudden laughter broke the spell I was under, and I began to laugh too. At the same moment, Sophie shouted, "A house! A house!" and ran. She was instantly out of sight. I followed.

No more than twenty yards away was a high granite wall, perhaps the back of a barn. We ran around the side and stopped. Above our heads, along the side wall of a still larger building opposite, were long lines of smashed windows. Glass crackled at our feet, and we had to pick our way cautiously over it. An overflow pipe dripped, the drops trickling off thick green slime. A kind of concrete vat, chipped around the rim and coated with sludge, caught the water and fed it out through a hole into tributaries of the stream. I ran forward, Sophie to the left, both of us scanning the ruins to see if a real living house were somehow attached. There was no one, nothing.

Then suddenly, marvelously, a voice!

"*Holà!*"

Male, fog-obscured.

"Where?" Sophie answered. "Where are you? Quick, we need help!"

"*Holà!*"

The voice again called us—a bit to the right.

"Hey! We're over here!" I yelled.

"*Holà. Venez!* Come on!"

A figure emerged into view, crunching glass underfoot. Tall, broad-shouldered, solid, the build of a big peasant farmer. Was it a shepherd's crook he was cradling? But, no. It wasn't a crook. It wasn't what a shepherd or a farmer would be carrying. Oh Christ! This man had a submachine gun at the hip, pointing at our middles.

The instant we saw what we'd stumbled into, we threw ourselves behind cover. Two shots sang into the granite and another whined out into the fog.

Christ! It was the Saki story . . . the two deadly enemies felled beside each other by a toppled tree in the forest, making friends when all but dead, seeing help distantly in the trees, coming closer, they cry out with joy, closer . . . but it is wolves.

Boots clamped on the shale. I pulled Sophie's hand and we tumbled back up the hill, silent on a patch of silky grass, into the cloud, invisible, gasping but without noise.

Another shot . . . random.

A whistle . . . more shouts. Fuck it! There were two of them, one above, one below. We were in a vise, and the handle needed only a quick twist. We plunged off at a tangent, desperate to escape the tightening grip. Another whistle.

"Gone left!"

We were hunted animals, and they had apparently spotted us. Should we fight on?

"Stop or I shoot!"

"Bluff!" Sophie whispered. "We can't see them, they can't see . . . ."

But they could. And we, suddenly, could see both of them.

"Don't move, Sophie," I said softly but urgently.

"Keep dead still and they won't fire." Maybe—I added to myself.

They said nothing until the sergeant-major was almost on top of us. He gave a low laugh, raised his gun, aimed at my heart. I flung myself sideways, my left arm flailed around and hit a rock, smashing my wrist watch. It was 1013.

"Just a warning," said the sergeant-major. His brother smiled, but a little sadly, as if he'd been deprived of something. "Now move! *Les deux—allez, 'op!*"

Chapter 6

December 15.   10:14 A.M.

THE SERGEANT-MAJOR loved the idea that we'd made a giant semicircle, starting from the cliff to the right of the mine, ending in the abandoned administration buildings down to the left of it. He and his brother had rendezvous'd there, ending their hunt. They had just decided to return to pick up the plutonium and rush it to Diélette, boat or no boat, to load it from the beach, if necessary. He told us all this happily, marching us on the double back to the mine and to the shed. Now, he said, they had half an hour's grace. It was the old plan again, wait at the mine for the 1100 tide. The commandant would be relieved.

145

Outside the shed, he paused a second. The door had been put back up. But it was hard to open it. "A friend of yours is in there, Ivan," he said, giving it a series of strong pulls. "He'll be glad to see you too. Another friend will be with you in a minute. It's okay, Popoff, you can let go her hand, she won't fall down. *Allez!*"

The door grated open and inside, indeed, was an old friend. His sickly color, green as a comic-book Martian, was so startling that for a second I refused to believe it really was Godfrey Mackeson-Beadle.

He waved a hand at me feebly, flopped against the far wall. Then he opened his mouth like a frog about to croak. "Out all night on that boat. Ghastly. Amanda . . . Amanda'll tell you."

"*Amanda?*" I managed to croak back at him.

The old man's lungs erupted in a fit of coughing, deep and thick. I remembered the desperate breathing of my uncle, dying of bronchitis in a post-war Moscow winter.

"Amanda?" I began again, in a calmer voice. But a scraping noise attracted my attention and my eye was suddenly caught by Sir Ronald Hisland standing in the doorway, letting the wind ruffle his hair and flap at his mackintosh. It didn't, however, affect the now familiar smug expression on his face. He produced a bottle of scotch and held it out for me to take.

"Damn fool, Gull. Lucky you and the girl weren't killed." Then to his old chum, "Rest up, Godfrey, and you'll be fine in no time. Your girl's all right, running repairs. Be in in a minute. See all's shipshape, sergeant-major, then have a quick word with me outside."

He left the sergeant-major inside to watch us and slammed the door. The bent wood shrieked but remained intact.

Sophie dropped to her knees, as appalled as I to see

anyone in such terrible physical shape. She took the bottle from me and handed Mackeson-Beadle a nip of scotch in the screw-top, which he accepted with alacrity.

"I am Sophie Bonnissent. I am with Vladimir."

"Ah! Thank you. Mercy beaucoop. Sorry about all this, I—" His words drowned in coughing.

"Later," I said. "Rest a little first." I was burning with curiosity to know what had happened to Mackeson-Beadle since he'd vanished from the *auberge*—and even more how Amanda'd got mixed up in it all. But it was useless to go too fast. The old man was in terrible shape.

"Trouble is, trouble is, there's not much time," said Mackeson-Beadle, panting hard, painfully. "One more sip and a minute to pull myself together. I can't . . ."

The effort was too much. He closed his eyes. I kept mine on him huddled in the dimness of the shed, a pile of wet tweed that virtually hid the man inside.

Sophie felt his forehead and made a face to me, as if to say she suspected a fever.

"No, no," a voice mumbled from the heap of clothes. "Not sick. Just . . . bedraggled."

I brought over a blanket. She took it and arranged it around his shoulders.

"Thanks. Better now."

He slumped back and almost at once began to snore, his breathing gradually becoming more easy and relaxed.

The sergeant-major laughed from his corner. "A night out at sea, the old man'll sleep like a clog."

But should I let him sleep, I wondered, if he had something urgent to say? He was right; there wasn't much time. And was Amanda really here somewhere?

147

Whether she was or not, even if the police did show up there was no reason now for them to suspect that Mackeson-Beadle was *not* the culprit, especially if the plutonium cages were already loaded onto his boat. What was the connection with Sir Ronald Hisland now? What was the line pointing to him? Apart from us!

I shivered. It wasn't entirely fear. My own clothes were still wet, slimy and cold.

The sergeant-major got to his feet. "All shipshape, then. I'll leave you alone," he announced. "But I shan't go far. So nothing stupid this time. No good trying to empty the sea with a teaspoon."

The door scraped open and shut again.

"*Zut!*" cried Sophie as soon as he'd gone, stabbing a finger in the direction of Mackeson-Beadle. "After what you told me, Vladimir, I had an outside, a very outside, bet on him."

Another snore escaped from beneath the wet and by now steaming lump. Then it shuddered, shook and began to rise at the center until Mackeson-Beadle's head popped into view, like one of those time-lapse films of plants bursting out of their seeds.

"Always feel better for forty winks," he declared in a much clearer, more confident tone.

"More like four winks," I said, "or four fingers," as he reached again for the bottle of scotch.

"My God, Vladimir," the old man said abruptly, "you look terrible. So does . . . so does . . . ?"

He had obviously forgotten.

"Mademoiselle Sophie Bonnissent," I supplied. "Nuclear expert. Got caught up in the hijack. We tried to get away. They shot Pierre."

"That chap Denis? Good God. Ronnie . . . he's gone too far. I say, I am most terribly sorry about all this. It's

148

absolutely all my fault." He looked around him. "Where's my poor old girl?"

"I don't know," I said. "Amanda hasn't . . . I think the sergeant-major went out to—"

"Sergeant-major?"

"Ronnie's right-hand man. The tough-looking guy with the crewcut who was in here a moment ago."

"Ah."

"But what happened?" I prompted him. "Is Amanda . . . ? How . . . ?"

Mackeson-Beadle gave a huge cathartic cough and ploughed on. "If I'd done my duty, I . . . If I'd not—"

"What happened?" I reminded him.

"Ah. Well, a chap came for me. Ronnie told me something of what's been going on here. While I was being . . . unloaded—" Another cough made him stop. "Absolutely frightful. I really must do something. Make amends. Quite mad." He paused to inhale deeply.

"Amanda?" I said again. "Begin from the beginning. Tell me about her."

Mackeson-Beadle groaned. "She went down to the yacht marina as she said she would. And damn it, she found me, as luck would have it. Wish she hadn't."

"You were moored in Cherbourg?"

"Well, this man was with me, you see. Remember, red-haired chap? We saw him in the harbor. Took me round there from Diélette. Found me at the back of the pub. He had to pick up these chaps in Cherbourg, so we both . . . He had, er, he had a gun. Poor old Amanda walked right in, sevenish last night. Nobody around, and . . . well, there we both were."

"And he took you both for a ride out to sea."

Mackeson-Beadle winced. "God, what a night! He was waiting for another one of that . . . that private army of Ronnie's. Then we pushed off. Got a bit rough then, you see. You must've heard the wind yourself. Brave girl, Amanda. But, er, I'm terribly afraid, old man, her . . . the little infant's gone. Very much afraid so."

I blinked. That was all. Shut my eyes once, quickly, and tried not to think more about it.

"Then we pulled into shore early this morning, you see. Very early, still dark. One got off. Later on these two *other* characters turned up. God knows where we were exactly, some little cove, but not all that far from here. They put some steel tubing stuff on board and took us off, brought Amanda and me up to where we are now. She's still out there with 'em, I suppose, poor girl. Up here at the mine, I mean."

He paused. The effort of speaking was telling on him.

"I'm not in great shape," he went on. "But she's worse, oh dear me. Not at all in good shape. I hope they're doing something for her out there. Poor old stick. Terribly upset. I mean about the . . . What a night!"

It became harder and harder to think about it, to draw conclusions. I wish I could be more proud of my first reaction, but it's just not something you can control. Amanda was sick, maybe in danger. Yet I thought first . . . I am free! I suppressed it. I was ashamed of it and fought it back. Did my face show any of it, did Sophie or Mackeson-Beadle himself notice? Hell, that wasn't what mattered.

Meanwhile Sophie was talking to the old man—in English, since the sergeant-major had gone.

"So there is nothing, no trail you have left which could upset Sir Ronald's story, which will make them believe it is not you, monsieur, but he? I am imagining the reaction outside. They read in the paper about this . . . organization on the island, a trail leads them to suspect you, who are missing. And when, sooner or later, they find your boat with the cages, they will believe the plutonium is on Guernsey, of course. How would it be possible to detect a crossing in this . . . *sale temps,* this dirty weather?"

"And if I never show up again? If . . . ?"

Sophie patted his hand. But she didn't deny what he implied. Her face was grim.

"*Zut!* Sir Ronald is in danger of succeeding, so to speak."

"Oh God, what have I—?" Mackeson-Beadle began again.

"Do you know anything about the FGM?" I asked him quickly, fearing he would exhaust himself unnecessarily over his guilt.

"Eh? FGM?"

"The Free Guernsey Movement. That's the flag Ronnie's fighting under."

"I don't know anything. I—" He coughed again violently.

"Don't worry, Mr. . . . Beetle. Not for yourself. There is a long way to go. How, for example, and to whom, is anyone to reply? I mean to say, is he going to dialog with the police? If so, that must be dangerous to him."

"I don't know at all," the old man muttered.

Sophie shook her head, seeing that he was going to be of little help. "*Quel bordel,*" she said with a groan.

"Pity I wasn't awake in time before the hijack," I said distractedly. "Otherwise I might have taken a tip from Hansel and Gretel."

"*Hein?* Oh, dropped bits of iron ore along the route!"

151

"Well, left something at the scene of the crime, anyway."

"Yes. But you weren't. And you didn't."

"No. Or maybe . . ."

"What?"

I said nothing. Of course there was no French Sherlock Holmes out there, sniffing the air, tracing the smell of Ronnie Hisland's Fox's mixture to half a dozen privileged customers, checking all their alibis, putting two and two together and . . . Oh, hell!

"Fog's lifting a bit," I said, just to say something that could not be disputed. It was true, because I could see just a bit more light in the sky through the dirty little window in the roof.

"*Vous savez . . .*" Sophie began, and she looked suddenly more animated, a flush on her downy, muddy cheeks and a sparkle of bright blue in her eyes. "I wonder if two can play at the hostage game?"

"Eh?" grunted the old man.

"I mean, the plutonium is here, we are not so heavily guarded now. Could we not use the radioactive material ourselves in some way to . . . to hold Mr. Hisland, Sir Ronald I mean, to say to the men with the guns: If you shoot, we kill your *patron,* your boss, we contaminate him?"

Her blue eyes glinted. She was a real fighter. I felt ashamed of my growing fatalism.

"The trouble is," she went on, her voice cold, precisely articulated, "there is almost no way of threatening him without threatening ourselves too."

"Even assuming," I said, "we can get near the stuff. This goddam shed is likely to be our tomb."

"Oh, I can find some excuse for approaching the canisters," she said quickly. "The thing is delay in any

152

case. The police *will* find the place. They will search the whole Cotentin and it cannot be long before they find us here. You and I may have lost an hour *and* our best chance out there in the fog, but the point is the same: we—and the plutonium—*must* still be here when they come. They must find us before, *well* before 1050, *or* we must find a way to stay here longer until they do."

I unscrewed the top of the scotch bottle and passed it around. We all swallowed some.

At the same time, I watched Sophie. And instead of trying to help her follow through her idea, I allowed my mind to go off on a tangent, to waste valuable time regretting the presence of Mackeson-Beadle, the presence, somewhere outside, of his daughter . . . of Amanda . . .

ALMOST AT once the mental image became the real thing. For there, suddenly, was Amanda. The sergeant-major and his brother stumbled into the shed, holding the four corners of a tattered gray blanket to make a stretcher. In it lay the woman I might have married. They lowered her, wrapped and all but invisible, to the floor, then let the coarse wool fall around her.

As her bottom hit the floor, she gasped, "Oh shit!"

There was some of the old self left.

She did indeed look in worse shape than her father, more yellowish-white than green, the color of old parchment, hollow-cheeked. Chestnut hair fell over her face, sticking to the skin, but with sweat not mud.

For a second she just lay there. The sergeant-major stood over her, as if to check that she had survived being dumped onto the floor; then he looked at the rest of us.

"Don't try and move the lady," he said.

153

"She's okay," said the brother. "No bones broken. I've checked." He sounded less than confident.

"She needs food, that's all. Stomach's in her heels," added the sergeant-major. "There's all you need in here. *Bien, ma cocotte,* you're back with daddy and your friends. Not so bad, huh?"

"Bugger off," said Amanda, still supine and motionless. The two men smiled and did as she said, slamming the door behind them.

"Darling, are you . . . ?" Old Mackeson-Beadle's voice cracked into a wheeze.

"Oh hello, daddy, are you here? I didn't see you. I didn't know whether those two bastards were joking. Don't worry about me, I'm okay. Hello, Vladimir. Pull me upright. Introduce me to your friend."

"No, don't move. Mademoiselle Sophie Bonnissent, Amanda Colville, Godfrey's daughter. Now, love, lie down. This isn't a debutante's ball. Let me get you some food."

"Hand me a cigarette if there're any around." She was shivering violently.

I took a pack of Players from a carton and opened it. Amanda pushed her lighter toward me and I lit one for her. She took it, pulled her knees up under the blanket, leaned her head back against the wall and inhaled deeply.

"Some holiday!" she said, letting the smoke stream out. "Why the hell didn't you tell me more on the phone, Vladimir?"

"Your father didn't want me to. Besides, I had no idea . . . ."

"Don't blame it all on daddy, for God's sake."

"My dear, I . . . ."

And Mackeson-Beadle again broke into a fit of coughing.

"I know just what you're thinking, Vladimir," Amanda said, "and for Christ's sake don't let's talk about it. Just tell me what your ideas are for getting us all out of here. I hope you've got some, because that's *all* I'm interested in." She winced and pulled herself back into the corner of the shed. She was in pain, but refused to compromise with it, refused to show it more than absolutely forced to by her reflexes. She had her faults but she was full of guts.

Sophie and I glanced at each other.

Amanda reddened. I recognized the first sign of that temper I had never yet learned to deal with, but Sophie was quicker on the uptake.

"I am sorry. Vladimir did not sufficiently introduce me. I am a nuclear physicist at La Hague. I was in the escort car when they hijacked the plutonium."

Amanda's stare changed to one of curiosity and sympathy. She smiled, thank God. "Yes, they told me something about that," she said with a sigh. "You mustn't mind what I say. I'm just a bit strung out, you know, *nerveuse.* Besides, it's Ronnie I'm really furious with, and he's not here for me to yell at. No, I'm damn glad you're here. For my sake, not for yours. At least *someone* knows the ins and outs of plutonium! But if you want anything new from me, you're going to be disappointed. They hardly told me a thing. The men on the boat kept quiet and waved their guns in my face. As a matter of fact, we were preoccupied with other, messier matters. I . . . ."

She had to catch her breath, putting the cigarette to her lips to disguise her pain, mental as well as physical.

"Yes," Sophie said softly. "I am sorry. But it's half

past ten. We have very little time. Please tell me, madame, anything you know. It could help."

"Bugger all, I'm afraid. I told you, they . . . ."

"What could you see out there just now?" I asked her quickly. "Are they getting ready to move out? What's going on outside right now?"

"Don't ask me, Vladimir," she said, cross again. "I was in the back of a van. Then in here. I think I heard someone say something about the *St. George* coming into Diélette to take them off. Could that be right?"

"Yes. In half an hour. Even less. What else?"

"Nothing. That's all."

"You know nothing of their plans for us?" I insisted.

"No, my dear. Nothing. How many times d'you want me to say it?"

After that I kept quiet. Seeing the two women together brought back the sinking feeling I remembered having so often when Amanda was around. I was afraid of her, of her temper, her bossiness, her shifts of mood. And the situation we were in now wasn't calculated to bring out the best in anybody.

Amanda went on, "Is that scotch?"

I passed it to her. She drank, then turned to Sophie.

"How did you know I was *madame,* by the way?? Has Vladimir . . . ?"

"No, not at all," said Sophie, with a laugh that had a very slight edge to it. "Vladimir was very . . . reticent. But how do I know you have been married? Because your name is Colville and your father's is . . . not."

"Of course. Silly of me."

"But you are not still married?"

"No, certainly not. And it looks as if I'm not going to be again. After all."

This conversation had gone on long enough. In Sophie's eyes, did any shred of my credibility remain? I waded in.

"Amanda, you said you weren't going to talk about that."

"No, Vladimir, but I can hint, can't I, allude, cast aspersions?"

"We hardly had the occasion—" began Sophie.

"Not for want of wanting. No, I know, he's a handsome wreck of a man, isn't he? I don't blame you for trying. Oh, hell!" She looked at me. "And how did you like Guernsey?"

"Algiers to a T."

"Bastard."

"Come," said Sophie sharply. "We are wasting time. We cannot allow—"

"I know. You're right. I'm sorry."

She subsided into the blanket, wrapping her arms around her stomach. I saw tears in her eyes. Her father was snoring almost imperceptibly by her feet.

"Pass me the scotch again," she said. "I still hurt like hell."

Sophie took the bottle over and knelt down beside Amanda, putting one hand on her forehead. She winced and drew in her breath. Then she pursed her lips as if she'd come to an important decision.

"You have a fever. Quite high, one hundred and four at least. I will speak to Sir Ronald." She stood up and motioned me to join her at the door. "She does indeed have a fever. But really I need an excuse to see Sir Ronald. An idea has come to me . . . if only I can get some kind of a bath."

"Bath? That's hardly likely . . . and you're not all that . . ."

She interrupted, but patiently. "No, I mean any bit

157

of water confined in a small space. Like we said, remember, if the plutonium . . . But I'll explain if I see any prospect of it working out."

She pushed the door open. I glimpsed the Welshman who'd missed so many of his dentist appointments standing guard between the shed and the bunkers behind. His head was bandaged messily, his nose inflamed. He swiveled, leveling his submachine gun, fearing a repeat performance. So I stayed inside the shed and called out that we needed to see Sir Ronald urgently.

"Yeah?" he said, eager to refuse the request but afraid to make decisions. He called out to brother Georges who came running over from the direction of the silos. They had a whispered conference. Sophie was called over. She made a series of points with fulsome gestures. Eventually the Welshman told me to come out too and walk slowly toward the tower. He stood back at a distance where he could watch the shed and at the same time see that neither Sophie nor I tried to run. Georges preceded us to the tower.

Inside the hall of the white tower Sir Ronald Hisland and the sergeant-major were in agitated discussion. They looked up, surprised.

"Says it's important," Georges said. "I've got to get down to the harbor."

"Mrs. Colville needs help," said Sophie quickly, walking right up to Sir Ronald, "but first there's an even more urgent technical matter. Please believe me it is no bluff this time. It is the health of all of us I am concerned to protect."

"What is this all about, mademoiselle?" Sir Ronald said quickly.

Using me as interpreter, she began to reel off technical information about the spontaneous overheating of

158

plutonium in a confined space and left uncooled for more than a very short time.

At the end, Sir Ronald got to his feet and looked at her suspiciously. "You mean, left as it is, it gets too hot. Needs to be cooled down from time to time. Right?"

"That is correct. During transport, it is kept at a distance from other solid matter. Hence the cages. On arrival in Paris, in the normal course of events, it would go into concrete casks with hollow tubes for water to flow continuously. Since it is still here, we must at once prepare a makeshift cooling bath. It will be quite easy." Sophie spoke with a real sense of urgency and professional concern. Even to me, knowing that she had something up her sleeve, it sounded plausible as hell. All the same it was surprising Ronnie was so easily . . . gulled. It made me wonder all over again just how precisely he had planned the whole operation. He seemed to have done virtually no homework and to have left a lot to chance. His madness no doubt explained it.

"Down there, the stairwell is already half full." Sophie, surveying the concrete shambles, pointed an imperious finger.

It was true. The night's continuous rain had channeled about two feet of water into the space where the steps led down to the iron door.

Sir Ronald looked at his watch. "It can wait half an hour."

"No, it can't. Not if you're going to be quite safe. Touch it and see."

Sir Ronald looked toward the nearest canister, ominously stenciled with orange radiation warnings, then thought better of it.

"We can use the stairwell," she went on, "but we need more water in it."

159

Sir Ronald again looked at his watch, then at the canisters. "I suppose," he said after some hesitation, "I suppose there's no harm in getting the cooling bath ready. Even if we don't have time to use it. All right. Gull, since you're here, get to work. Give him a hand, sergeant-major."

At once we began rushing around collecting scraps of ragged canvas and five or six of the less rotten planks that littered the floor. I rammed these into the cracks around the iron door. My legs, already numb, hardly reacted to being immersed again. The sergeant-major found a rusty tub over by the chute. Sir Ronald himself helped haul it to the pit to tip a few gallons of filthy water into the mixture of rain water and alluvial slime already in the bath. At the end the commandant was puffing hard.

Sophie took advantage of their labors to get in a quiet word with me.

"They're building their own trap," she whispered. "If the plutonium gets in there, it'll be deadly. Water acts like anything else that comes too close to the canisters. Remember we talked about it on the cliff. The particles can't escape. They start bouncing back and out again, back and out again. Very fast. If we could only threaten Sir Ronald, suspend him over it. . . ."

"I follow. But will the others—?"

"Get on with it, Gull," boomed Sir Ronald's voice from the other end of the tower, where he was peering at the furthest of the canisters over the top of a hunk of concrete. He seemed to have caught the spirit of urgency that Sophie and I were manufacturing. "Be prepared, eh? Not that I expect to use it. Off any minute. Mademoiselle will no doubt advise us again when we get on board."

I jammed another plank into the stairwell, wondering if that meant we might all be taken off on the *St. George.* Or was that too much to hope for?

"That's it, Number Five!" the commandant yelled out.

The job was done. The pit was thigh-deep in water.

Sir Ronald gestured toward the Welshman who was standing in the open doorway. "Take Gull back. I'll look after the girl."

Hell! The last thing I wanted was to get separated from Sophie at this stage. The whole point was to take out Ronnie, to use his life as a bargaining counter, and we hadn't been able to discuss how we were going to do it. Should I try some heroics now? I glanced at Sophie . . . helplessly. She seemed calm. She always did. Did she think she could handle it alone? There was nothing else to do except make a smart about turn.

Outside, the sea-fog was a little more patchy than before but showed no signs of disappearing. There was no longer that claustrophobic nighttime sense of being wrapped in a sodden coal sack. The sun was rising behind there somewhere; perhaps it had even reached above the level of the cliff by now. It could break through.

I stretched my hands above my head and yawned loudly, trying to procrastinate, to hang around by the door, to think of something, some diversion, before I went back to the prison cell in the shed, back to the almost routine role—by now—of Greek chorus.

In fact, that second's delay in the open doorway was vital.

I don't know if they saw me first, or I saw them.

Bob Hardacre, Don Gaffney and Claire Fouquet.

Of course! Laden with cameras and bags of fog filters,

they were coming to get those shots of the mine, the shots that Pierre had persuaded them to get back during yesterday's lunch at the *auberge*. They must have become a bit suspicious about where their guide had got to and come up to scout the location themselves. They were walking slowly up the track alongside the sea wall, three abreast. From his gestures, I could tell that Don Gaffney was in the middle of one of his elaborate technical demonstrations for the benefit of Bob Hardacre. Claire, squeezed between them, was looking straight ahead.

It was she who suddenly stopped and pointed. "Vladimir!"

The girl's voice cut the mist like a cheese-wire. The Welshman turned, swore, shoved the barrel of his submachine gun in my spine and propelled me back into the tower.

"People! Saw the bastard. Knew who he was," he yelled.

Sir Ronald gaped.

But the sergeant-major reacted with the speed of a commando. He charged outside, gun at the ready.

Even so, he was too late. "Where? Where the hell did you see 'em?" he shouted back in our direction, his eyes searching the fog in desperation.

The Welshman, dripping sweat and saliva, ran out again. I followed. There was no sign of any of the three members of the film crew. Good, they had seen the gun.

"Get the police!" I shouted as loud as I could into the fog. The soggy air muffled my yell.

"*Écrase!*"

But the sergeant-major didn't hang around to shut me up. Instead he ran down the path toward the road to Diélette, the path they'd have to take to reach help. Unless they went up the cliff. It wasn't impossibly steep at that point. But how quick were they? On the uptake as well as on their feet? And Claire undoubtedly in high heels!

I could do nothing but hope to hell they would read the situation right and get to the police.

Then I heard a shot.

THAT WAS the worst moment. Ever since I'd had the idea of coming over to France things had gone wrong. Pierre was dead. Amanda and her father were prisoners and sick. Sophie Bonnissent was also a prisoner . . . in the tower. She was there now beside me, leaning against a pillar, smudging a slogan that said *"Fais l'amour, pas la guerre!"* And now the film crew, having barely escaped drowning, were being hunted down by a man with a submachine gun in a state of undeclared war against anyone who threatened his "operation."

And yet, outside, there was no more shooting. Just that one report, half-deadened by the fog.

I moved to the doorway to get a view down the path, but Sir Ronald was vigilant. He waved his pistol at me.

"Damn interfering . . . " he began.

But the sergeant-major careened in, cutting him off, charging the white tower like an infuriated rhino. "Move out!" he yelled. "Get this stuff loaded. Forget the fucking tide!"

Sir Ronald was beginning to look frightened.

"Did you find 'em, sa'ant-major?"

"No. Thought I did, took a shot down the path, but the bastards must've gone up the cliff."

Sophie and I smiled at each other.

"Where the hell's Georges?" the sergeant-major shouted.

163

I suddenly realized just how shorthanded they were. Georges had gone to Diélette to rendezvous with the *St. George,* Ronnie's boat. The others had taken the cages to load them onto Mackeson-Beadle's boat and weren't back, probably weren't due back. The Welshman was still here, but no one was guarding Amanda or her father. Not that they could be much of a threat —or help—to me in the state they were in.

Yet, just as I was putting the odds at somewhere near even, they tipped back in Ronnie's favor.

The Simca drove up and squealed to a halt by the silos outside. Georges got out and ran into the tower.

"Okay!" he shouted, beaming. *"Foutons le camp!* The boat's just outside the harbor!"

Sir Ronald sagged a moment with relief, then quickly pulled himself together. "Right. Load the plutonium. That means you, Gull. *And* the young lady. Get the car ready. Scramble!"

"You're crazy," I said. "It's suicide to pick those things up in our hands. Sophie, tell him!"

Sir Ronald was not in a mood to debate the point. He made a show of patting the cumbrous German pistol in his pocket, cocking it. "Pick the bloody stuff up, man, and load it in the car!"

Again I had no choice.

I moved to the nearest canister behind its protective slab of concrete. Sir Ronald walked a couple of steps behind me to make sure I obeyed.

Two steps too near.

For that was my only choice now—play the hero.

I snatched at the canister. With the same movement I flung it hard. It caught Sir Ronald on the right knee, skidded and hit the water behind him. The bath, that fatal bath!

He howled with pain, teetered on the edge, regained his balance, swung around.

Sophie's first reaction was to duck. A split second later she diverted the Welshman by dashing for the door. "Look out!" she screamed in a frightened voice calculated to give everyone pause.

The sergeant-major—like the Welshman when Pierre had made his bid—was split between two scenes of action. Fearing for his own safety, he was too slow—in fact he had no chance—to get a share of either.

Sophie, still making a show of concern over the stability of the plutonium, surrendered to the Welsh guard, then to Georges, who'd run back in.

But I was already behind Ronnie with my right arm tight around his neck. "That water's a death trap," I yelled at the same time. "Move or shoot and the boss goes in."

The sergeant-major, thank God, hesitated and stepped back.

The old knight in my arms made a token attempt to get free. But I crooked my elbow even harder around his neck. He gagged and went still.

We were both out of breath. But there was no doubt who was in charge.

"The water's already poisonous enough to kill. If you don't believe me, ask the expert."

The sergeant-major and I both turned our heads. He in the direction of Sophie, I toward the bath behind me.

The water looked innocent enough, dirty, of course, with the muck from the floor and walls, but that was nothing compared to the deadly plutonium bombarding it from down there at the bottom of the pool.

"Ask her," I repeated, breathlessly. "Ask her. Anyway, it's bloody obvious if you know the first thing about the stuff."

"Georges!" the sergeant-major shouted. "Keep her covered."

The brother's gun swung around.

The sergeant-major's own submachine gun jerked upward a degree and pointed at Sir Ronald's throat.

"*Merde!*" the brother exclaimed. Then, "For Christ's sake, what're you waiting for? The bastard hasn't even got a gun!"

Which reminded me. I hadn't.

But as long as Ronnie couldn't get at it, that gun of his was better off in his pocket than in my hand. If the sergeant-major got the impression I was threatening *him* and was about to shoot him, he wouldn't be fussy then about winging his commanding officer at the same time as he shot me. I preferred to stick to our chosen weapons, his gun and my plutonium. Equal deterrence was a safer bet than trying to win the arms race by starting the war.

Sir Ronald jerked his head back and forth. His mouth gaped—but no sound came out. His face was white with fear, or maybe lack of oxygen.

What next? I couldn't stay here forever. What could I hope to bargain for? The vital thing was that Sir Ronald Hisland should come out of his coma and plead for himself . . . even though that meant loosening my grip. But first I wanted to have him hear Sophie's explanation of the dangers he faced.

So just for now I kept my forearm clamped firmly across his vocal cords.

"Persuade them, Sophie love," I said. "Persuade them just how deadly that pool is here. They saw the plutonium go in."

Sophie looked at me for a moment, her mouth shut tight, her blue eyes flashing. "I may as well tell you directly, Sir Ronald," she began. "In English."

"*Salope!*" muttered the sergeant-major, barely suppressing the urge to make a grab for her. "*Béchamel!*"

"The water sets up a process whereby the alpha particles cause a fission reaction, releasing neutrons which first give rise to what we call the Cerenkov effect, whereby—"

Sir Ronald was desperately trying to say something, so I decided to let him. I think he'd got the drift.

"Don't . . . don't let 'em . . . sa'ant-major. Argh! God damn it, man, he's got us by the balls."

I gave his neck a tweak to get his anatomy straight.

"Leave me. Clear out while you can."

He stopped, gasping for breath.

"Very heroic," I said. "Now tell the troops they can bugger off. Fast. Now. Just so long as they leave the plutonium right where it is. Tell them to go play hide-and-seek with the police and good luck to them. There's nothing for them to do here."

"Get going," he said in a kind of throaty whimper . "I . . . ."

"Tell 'em, Ronnie," I said.

"I . . . ."

But he stopped when he saw the sergeant-major and his brother putting their heads together and consulting in quick low voices. When at the end they made no move to go, he began again.

"Get a move on. Let me . . . ."

Sweat was pouring down his face, now scarlet with the returning blood and the effort.

A cramp was setting in my right arm.

Then something happened that sent a flash of panic

through me, something worse than a physical counter-attack.

A self-satisfied grin spread over the sergeant-major's face. The pupils of his eyes seemed to dilate, visibly. He ran his hand through his cropped hair and rubbed the back of his bull neck voluptuously.

Sir Ronald watched all this happen, too, without understanding. "Go on, man," he whispered hoarsely. "Don't let . . . ."

But I had a horrible feeling . . . .

"Okay, Vladimir," said the sergeant-major suddenly. "Toss the bugger in. You didn't believe me, did you? Neither did he. I told you, though. It's me that pees on the wall 'round here. It's me that's the boss. The real boss, the big *mec*. That sparrow-head there"—he jabbed his gun in Sir Ronald's direction—"can take a bath whenever he likes. *Compris?* Thanks for your help, Sir Duchenoque, but we'll carry on. *Hein,* Georges?"

At the end of this weird speech—a speech I'd seen coming, but too late, too damn late—Sir Ronald Hisland tried to grunt out something, couldn't, then slumped in my arms like a child playing dead. I had to push his body sideways to prevent it from slipping, by itself, into the radioactive pit.

"Don't waste your sympathy," the sergeant-major spat at me, prodding me at the same time to the back of the tower. "Of course I led him round by the end of his nose. He was just a cover for the real thing. Mr. Moneybags. Free Guernsey Movement! *Ouf!* When it comes to plutonium, people swallow any story, they're so scared shitless. You too, you dumb bastard. But he got a kick out of being the 'commandant', he did—he, *Sir* Ronald!

168

He's still k.o.'d. He can't hear nothing. But . . . *merde* . . . you lot nearly massacred the operation. When he told me he'd made a bet, Christ, a bet! And that the other old guy and a Russki were coming over . . . I should've taken over then. Except I needed him to take the rap if the hijack had screwed up. Georges, get the gun out of the old fossil's pocket and get rid of it. Piece of old German junk. No bloody good messing along with private armies if you don't understand soldiers, *hein?*"

Georges laughed dutifully as he pulled the World War II vintage revolver from Sir Ronald's jacket pocket and tossed it into the plutonium pool. He pointed at me. "Fetch!" And burst out laughing.

The brother was turning out to be a real humorist too, God help us.

"So now," said the sergeant-major, relaxing, as if he'd forgotten temporarily that the boat was down there in the habor waiting and the *flics* combing the Cotentin for the hijackers, "so now we take the plutonium, the stuff that isn't in the water there, and clear out. Many months later maybe you'll read in your papers about a ransom that's been paid. That's if the operation goes wrong. If it goes right, and it will, you'll hear nothing. *Rien.* The money'll be paid, the police'll say zero, the populations'll live their peaceful lives not knowing nothing about it. You are quite ignorant who we are. We'll never ever see each other again. *C'est bien simple.*"

"And the others?" Sophie asked.

"They are gone, mademoiselle. They have been paid. Find 'em if you can. Hey, *toi!*"

The Welshman guarding the door, who had been listening with impassive sulky eyes, stiffened.

"Get the cords from the Simca. Bring the girl and the old man."

The Welshman went off in dumb obedience. I had the feeling events were moving altogether too fast for him.

"*Allez, vite!*" the sergeant-major shouted when he was already well out of view.

"Georges, back up the car."

The brother ran out.

Mackeson-Beadle and his daughter filed in seconds later, the Welshman half-escorting, half-dragging Amanda.

Both old men were by now in much the same dilapidated state. Mackeson-Beadle slumped in a damp tweedy heap on the floor beside Sir Ronald. Amanda's eyes were red with pain but she was concentrating to avoid showing it.

"Hey! *La fille!* And you, Ivan! Over here!"

The sergeant-major flung his arm in our direction.

"There are three tins of plutonium . . . here, here . . . and over there. Don't imagine I'm going to take any more risks with that *merde* than the old man there. As you were! Get 'em loaded! But with a little more care." He laughed. Georges laughed too. They reminded me of the cat and the fox in Pinocchio, the brother echoing the more obvious villainies of the senior partner. "Okay! *Allez! Vite!* Move! All of you!"

Sophie and I looked at each other, then out at the gray walls, the gray wet air, the ruined iron mine. *La ronde.* We'd played this infernal scene before. I felt tired, hungry, wet, filthy and in a state of nervous depression. Plutonium! If only the stuff had never been manufactured. Mother Nature was innocent in that respect. The buoyancy of the last few minutes of violent action had collapsed, leaving me feeling like the two old men looked.

We were back to square one—a nasty death by radiation the best we could hope for. The best? A quick bullet would be far better.

"Surely there's something round here we can use to handle it so we don't get too close," Sophie said, still searching for practical solutions, still remembering that time was on our side. She stopped, turned toward the sergeant-major. "Where's that gas trolley, isn't it—?"

But she never finished her sentence. At that moment Georges came into sight, reversing the Simca like a demented stock-car racer right up to the door of the white tower. He leaped out, his face creased with fear and fury.

"*Les flics!* Hundreds of them! All round the fucking mine!"

THE SERGEANT-MAJOR shoved us back out of the doorway. Georges, last in behind us, cannoned into the Welshman who tied himself in knots with the ropes he was carrying. All the men unslung their guns. The sergeant-major pulled the door shut. It provided terrible protection, just a frame crossed and recrossed by strands of barbed wire. All the same it acted like a net curtain; people outside couldn't see us inside, but we could see them. Through this screen—and over the roof of the Simca abandoned just beyond—I spotted figures in black uniforms popping up then disappearing behind cover right up on the crest of the cliffs.

Almost at once a voice on a loudspeaker filled the mine, echoing around the concrete walls of the white tower in which we huddled. "Throw away your guns. Come out in single file. Hands in the air."

They'd found an English speaker. They knew, then,

we were supposed to be the desperadoes of the Free Guernsey Movement.

Amanda and the commotion woke the two old men. Sir Ronald continued to lie on the damp concrete as if he'd had a stroke. But his chum perked up, got to his feet and gave a cheer.

Georges swung around at him and glared, nothing more.

"Y'see, Ronnie," Mackeson-Beadle growled, squatting beside him again, shaking him by the shoulder, "y'see! Stupid old fool. I told you they knew how to look after the stuff. There's your proof. Bloody old fool."

Amanda pulled at her father's jacket and hissed at him to be quiet. Mackeson-Beadle gave up trying to rouse Ronnie and sat peacefully beside her. He was smiling—but vacantly, as if preoccupied.

"Wait, daddy," she said. "It's not over yet."

"Throw away your guns. Come out in single file. Hands in the air."

The voices penetrated like a foghorn. But through the barbed-wire door there was no sign of the body that produced it, nor now of any other policemen.

Suddenly a burst of fire erupted like a sputtering Catherine wheel out on the cliffs. But there was no noise of bullets inside the tower. They were firing in the air, letting us know the score.

The sergeant-major and his brother looked at each other.

They had been checking their guns and ammunition, and appeared to be ready for something . . . They acted calmly, trained to cope coolly with a crisis. Had they rehearsed the next scene?

"Well? Eh? Tell me now, eh?"

The third man, the Welshman, suddenly began to

scream at them, face muscles twitching convulsively. Maybe he'd cut rehearsals. Certainly his nerves had never recovered from the stunning blow dealt him by Pierre. With the hand that wasn't clutching his gun he untangled himself fumblingly from the ropes he had been carrying and began fingering the bloodstained bandage on his head.

"Well, what the hell d'we do now, eh?"

The sergeant-major muttered something to his brother which nobody else could catch. He ignored the yelling Welshman.

"Well, eh, for Christ's sake?"

The small man screamed again, the black stumps of his teeth gleaming wetly in his mouth. The bandage floated from his head like a party streamer. For a moment I thought he might turn his gun on the sergeant-major and his brother, but those two were watching him like hawks, their own guns at their hips.

"Come *on* . . ."

Seeing finally that no one was going to take the blindest bit of notice, he felt driven to act. He wrenched open the door of the tower. As the bandage fluttered to the ground, he jumped into the white Simca parked just outside, sliding straight into the driver's seat. The solid metal car body screened him at first from the policemen's view. But as soon as his head appeared behind the steering wheel, the bullhorn blared.

"You! Stop!"

Then another voice, unamplified but nearer.

"Arrêtez-vous!"

The loudhailer started to scream at him in both languages. But with no effect.

"Stooooop!"

"Haaaaalte!"

173

The Welshman roared the motor into life. The Simca jerked forward, reversed, then shot forward again. At that moment Georges ran toward the doorway. Taking advantage of his maneuver and the general preoccupation with the Welshman, I moved quickly to my right to a point where I could just see, at an angle, down the path toward Diélette.

What I witnessed was suicide induced by sheer panic.

The Welshman's first action was to smash the windscreen with the barrel of his gun and open fire everywhere, at everything—seagulls, granite walls, fog, maybe even some *flics*. I saw his gun blazing like a six-shooter in a movie while, with his other hand, he tried to steer the careening Simca. His mouth was open, screaming. But his howl was lost in the furious noise of the firing.

Georges, either out of anger or the irresistible sport of it, fired a burst himself at the Simca's rear end, then added a final couple of shots out toward the cliff.

Yet despite everything, for just a moment I thought the Welshman was going to make it through the encircling ring of policemen.

But when the *flics* fired back, they fired neither out of panic nor, like Georges, for the hell of it, but with the marksman's cool intent to kill. So many bullets hit the Welshman that he exploded like a pheasant shot by an elephant gun. The car actually buckled and bent, pieces of metal and rubber and plastic spinning off it like sparks from a Catherine wheel. It was a wreck before it even hit the sea wall.

I last saw the car's remains poised in the air over the rocks below, suspended as it were above the furnace. Then it plummeted out of sight.

Georges turned around at the same moment, saw me,

and angrily waved me back to my former position beside Mackeson-Beadle.

Then, turning again, he noticed through the doorway a *flic* running toward the point where the car had gone over the sea wall. I saw the man too. Teeth bared, Georges at last found a target he really wanted to hit. Ducking and weaving, the policeman ran for the wall's protection. But he never made it. Georges, grinning like a maniac, knocked him over with a single shot, two yards short of cover. The *flic* twitched once, then was still. Georges laughed. The sound echoed round the white tower.

Christ, I thought to myself, I hope they keep their nerves under control out there on the cliff. In here, there's little hope of sanity.

It was precisely then that a flicker of red caught my eye, a smell of burning rubber came at me from behind. I backed up a couple of paces to get a view of the spot where the Simca had finished up. The iron chute acted as a view-finder down onto that very section of rocks where the car had dived. But there was no water below now. The tide was still too far out. The dive ended in the disintegration of car and man.

A stink of burning rubber and seaweed curled up through the chute.

"The rest of you! Throw away your guns! Come out in single . . . ."

Two ear-splitting stereophonic rounds of fire from inside the tower drowned out the last words from the loudspeaker.

I whirled around.

At the doorway, Georges had fired another defiant burst in the direction of the cliffs. What the sergeant-major had done was much stranger. He had burst away the door at the bottom of the stairwell that had held the plutonium bath.

The water emptied in a rush, as if a giant plug had been removed. The canister of plutonium tumbled down one further step in the flow of debris and water, then caught on a piece of rotting wood, sticking at the top of what looked, now the padlocked door had swung open, like a long flight of stairs leading down to the sea and to the seams.

Was there a way out of the mine down there, for God's sake? Could one still get down to the seams and . . . out? Weren't they flooded even when the tide went out?

The sergeant-major said urgently to his brother, "Georges! Keep the bastards quiet five more minutes. Then I'll come for you. Watch the Russki. Keep 'em all over there." He jerked his head toward the old men.

Sophie and I joined them, guided by the tip of the gun-barrel.

The sergeant-major ran to one corner and rummaged in the heap of oxyacetylene cutters, coats, coils of rope and miscellaneous tools that were stored there, turned up a flashlight, glared back at us, knowing that his eyes were enough warning, and ran down into the pit.

We waited.

The smell of the smoldering car filled our concrete prison. There were muffled shouts outside. Now and then the loudspeaker blared out a message, and each time Georges fired a burst. There was no returning fire.

And all the while Georges kept his head flicking back and forth, watching us, watching the cliffs, watching us, in a regular rhythm.

"What happens down there?" I asked Sophie softly. She shrugged. "It must go down to the galleries, to the old seams. But it's flooded now, I'm sure. There can't be a way out. At least I think not."

"Even at low tide?"

"I think. In any case, it's rising fast."

"If he can get out," I said to reassure myself, "the police'll know where any tunnel comes out again. They can keep a watch there and he'll be no better off than a rabbit coming up just where the hunter's waiting."

"What he'll do in any case," Sophie said quietly, "is take hostages. That means you and me."

"I've been thinking that too. Can we stop them?"

"Not while they have the guns."

A bullet suddenly whanged against a concrete stanchion on the other side of the tower, ricocheted off and struck the iron chute like a Rangoon gong.

"*Merde!*" exclaimed Georges, who had got his rhythm wrong and fired a round inside the tower by mistake.

"Shit!" muttered Amanda, and pulled her coat tighter around her. "For Christ's sake do something, Vladimir!"

"I'm still hoping I won't have to," I snapped back.

The loudspeaker kept up its constant appeal for us all to come out quietly. Then suddenly the sergeant-major appeared on the double. He was frowning. That was *something*.

"*Venez,* mademoiselle! No, Popoff, I said 'mademoiselle.' "

His eyes caught mine. I saw a look I wouldn't have expected from him—worried, even frightened.

"I'll take care of her. *Allez! Vite!*"

Sophie walked as slowly as she dared over to the sergeant-major. He shone the beam of his flashlight at the pit. Having got a thumbs-up sign from Georges in reply to his own questioning look, he prodded Sophie down the stairs. She took care to step as far as possible to one side of the canister, lying apparently derelict but in fact as invisibly active as ever, just below the shot-away door. The sergeant-major, however, gave the plutonium a prod with his gun. I heard it rattle on down some more steps. Then they all—the man, the woman and the canister—dropped out of sight.

Georges kept up his vigil, while outside the loud-speaker appeals seemed to have ceased. There was a sudden quiet.

I did nothing, could do nothing, thinking of Sophie down there.

It was old Mackeson-Beadle who made the next move.

It took a moment for me to realize what he was doing. He had been virtually hidden behind Sir Ronald and Amanda and his damp coat. Now he was shuffling back-ward, leaving his coat propped against a lump of con-crete, working his way toward a slogan-covered pillar but stopping every time Georges turned in our direc-tion.

In the split second that he could afford us each time he turned, Georges didn't notice that anyone was edg-ing away from the group.

When Mackeson-Beadle saw that I had seen him, he put a finger to his lips. He gave me a look as if to say that he wasn't going to be deprived of his retribution, or his moment of glory. He was in one of his action phases again.

I gave him a look back that tried to say: "Be careful!"

At the same time I shifted my own body slightly to the left to help block Georges's line of view. Whatever Mackeson-Beadle planned to do, it was better than waiting passively. Besides, trying to stop him now would only call attention to his move.

Amanda saw what was going on and bit her lip. She looked at me reproachfully, as if I should have a monopoly of the heroics—and the danger—but she said nothing. I tried to get an unspoken message across that though her dad might be a social anachronism, I knew his heart was in the right place.

When Georges was busy with the outside again and I could safely turn around, Mackeson-Beadle had disappeared. Now, provided the sergeant-major didn't come back too soon . . . .

Sir Ronald groaned and began to come to. *Gospodi!* If only he would stay inert at this point . . . .

Suddenly my eye was caught by Godfrey Mackeson-Beadle reappearing just a couple of yards behind Georges. In his right hand he held a section of that barley-sugar iron which reinforces concrete walls, half again as long as his arm. The man with the submachine gun was back in his established pattern, peering out at the cliffs, then in at us, but never turning right around for fear of wasting a split second of observation time.

Godfrey Mackeson-Beadle drew back his arm.

Georges did a quick eyes-right to study the cliffs.

The old man stepped a pace forward and slammed down the iron bar.

The brother slumped to the ground, blood gushing from the side of his head.

Georges hadn't even hit the floor before I hurled myself forward to seize his gun. The sling got caught under his armpit as he fell, and I had to wrench it free. As I did so, his body did a flip-turn like a performing seal, then slammed back onto the muddy concrete floor. Amanda staggered across to her father who had gone deathly pale and was propping himself up against a wall, breathing like a marathon winner.

We had the whip hand now, except for Sophie who remained down in the pit with the sergeant-major. I still had to be careful.

I spun around. "Tell the police to get in here! Fast!"

I had shouted the instruction at Amanda. But she was already tugging the wire door open, bent double in pain though she was.

The timing of that shout of mine was terrible.

The sergeant-major's head snapped into view in the stairwell just as I yelled the word: "Fast!" I saw him at the very moment he saw the body of his brother Georges, stretched out and bleeding profusely. The sergeant-major froze. I brought up the submachine gun, but too late. He ducked out of view, leaving behind, like the Cheshire cat, an expression of horror that remained where his face had been. But I couldn't have fired. For all I knew, Sophie was just behind.

"Get behind cover!" I shouted again, this time to Mackeson-Beadle.

For Amanda was already outside and safe, and Sir Ronald—not that I cared about him at this point—was immobile.

As for me, I'd put some concrete between myself and the stairwell even before handing out the advice to others. But the sergeant-major's head didn't reappear.

Instead, I heard the rattling sound of a steel bottle bouncing down more stone stairs; then a metallic clang rang out. The canister as it fell emitted a hollow multiple echo . . . as if from the bottom of a very deep well.

Chapter 7

December 15.   11:45 A.M.

THE FIRST two policemen came in shoulder to shoulder at a run, split, and flung themselves behind cover. One yelled *"Okay!"* and a flood of black-uniformed, masked, shielded, heavily armed men poured into the white tower. They were crack CRS troops, the paramilitary shock force of the Ministry of the Interior.

I was glad they were on my side.

A middle-aged man with his visor up, teeth white and regular underneath a neat black mustache, ran up to me.

"Monsieur Gull?"

"Yes."

"Outside."

"Okay. But tell your men not to go down those stairs. There's only one guy left. But he's down there armed. He's got Mademoiselle Bonnissent with him."

"*Bien.*" The officer gave instructions, seized my arm and dragged me out into the wet midday.

"Get an ambulance," I said in mid-propulsion. Then I saw two ambulances parked fifty yards down the road to Diélette. "Fine. Madame Colville and her father need hospital care. Check them for radioactive contamination. And the lady has had a miscarriage. She needs a doctor fast. Do what you like with Sir Ronald Hisland —he's not going to deny anything. But the other one, the one down there, he turns out to be the boss. Have you got his brother?"

"That one?"

I turned toward a stocky, bloodstained, barely breathing figure propped by the open doorway to the white tower. A man in a white coat was examining his head. I nodded. "That's the one. Georges. There are others, but not here."

I told him that somewhere along the cliff Mackeson-Beadle's boat had been loaded with the empty cages; that two men were probably aboard her now out in the Passage de la Déroute. He gave more instructions. I mentioned the *St. George* nosing its way into Diélette harbor. He nodded, as if he knew about that.

Then I asked him, "Did you see the three film people?"

"Yes. But they only confirmed what we'd already guessed."

"Oh?"

"The body of a hijacker was found in the abandoned truck. We could not do a full examination for there were

182

signs of contamination. But there were traces of iron ore in the crevices of the soles, as well as a trace where a man's boot had been dragged on the road near the scene of the hijack."

"Good God!"

"But your film friends made it sure and allowed us to act at once."

"Good God!" I repeated, still thinking about the traces of ore. "Hansel and Gretel after all."

"Hein?"

"Nothing."

"We haven't got the others yet. When we do we'll need your help for identification."

"Okay," I said. "But let's get Sophie out of there first."

"Where's the rest of the plutonium?"

"Three of the canisters are shoved into corners in the tower. I hope to hell your men haven't . . . ."

The officer looked back toward the tower. One of his brighter lieutenants had seen to it that the place had been searched and the danger removed. The CRS were no bunch of Mr. Plods. I saw two men in spacesuits loading the foul stuff into a kind of mobile bank vault. Two more came into the tower with what I took to be meters to measure radioactive contamination.

"What's the name of the one still down there?"

"Name? Ah . . . the sergeant-major we called him. No one ever gave him a proper name. Better ask Georges."

"Georges is not available to be asked. He is too occupied dying."

Ambulances had already fetched the invalids; they had already taken my never-to-be father-in-law away. Amanda had gone too. They . . . and my past, I decided.

"The old man exaggerated with his blow," said the

officer. "That may have been our only chance of a coun-
ter-hostage. *Tant pis.* "

"You could still use him."

"Not if he can't speak. No proof then he's alive. No
value. But the *mec* down there will come out. He has
nowhere else to go."

"There's no way out, then?"

"Secret passages?" The officer laughed. "No, monsieur. Two of my men once worked in this mine. We
know it well."

"But Sophie—"

"If he keeps a gun on her, we'll let them both go,
unless we can get a clear shot at him. We'll see she
comes to no harm." He looked at me challengingly and
I wondered if I measured up. "They won't get far," he
went on. "He'll have to lose her soon enough. Do not
worry, Monsieur Gull. We have been through these
situations enough times before. Our tactics are well
studied."

"I hope your textbooks cover someone who has a
canister of plutonium as well as a gun and a hostage."

The officer glared at me. He was a pale-faced man, his
regulation mustache, cut straight along the of the upper
lip with a thin dividing line in the cleft beneath the nose,
proclaimed the ex-patrolman. A look like the one he
gave me was enough to make anyone reach for their
driving license.

"Wait here."

He went off to give more orders and find out what
was going on in the tower, leaving me to my thoughts,
such as they were, amid the commotion of the banging
doors of police *tubs,* shouts, roaring engines and all the
other brouhaha of a large-scale police maneuver. I felt
disoriented, suddenly alone in this crowd. The next few

hours and days, maybe weeks, would no doubt be a nightmare of depositions and statements, reconstructions and accusations. Even the sinking of that damn yacht probably still had to be accounted for.

Suddenly I wished, with absolute sincerity, that the sergeant-major had taken *me* down there, not Sophie. The thought surprised me, but as I stood there alone she was that precious to me. Not that I'd *want* to be held hostage in what must be a vilely dark, narrow, musty shaft with nothing at the bottom but the flooded seams and galleries of an abandoned mine. Self-sacrifice isn't a normal instinct of mine. I wouldn't have believed it possible that the urge to change places with her could be more than superficial and fleeting. But now it wasn't either. I felt it deeply, and the feeling wouldn't go away. It was the same feeling I'd had out in that bloody fog, strong counter-signals as tenderness and lust fought for priority. Now, mingled, they added almost up to love. If *she* were my wife . . . .

Well?

I knew I was not going back to Amanda. Amanda knew it too. What if? Maybe Sophie was looking for a Mr. Right. Even better, a Mr. Wrong with compensating qualities—understanding, with independent interests, not too young, but loving. Maybe, after this was over, I'd ask her if radioactive Russians could apply?

I heard a shout from inside the tower.

"HE'S CALLING for you," said the officer with the neat moustache.

"The sergeant-major? For me?"

I came nearer, right into the tower, and heard the voice myself.

"Hey, Gull, get down here! Send Russkoff down! Send him—or I shoot the doll."

It sounded far away, as if it had zigzagged up a narrow shaft from hell.

"Up to you," said the officer with apparent indifference, although in fact watching me closely. "He won't shoot her for that. I don't believe it. I can say you have been taken to the hospital with the other girl and the old men."

I hadn't expected to be taken at my word so soon.

But the idea had been to replace Sophie, not join her. All the same, that was better than staying up here, not knowing what she was facing, yet knowing she was down there with that bastard. Wasn't it? Anyway, I had no choice. If I declined, if I put Sophie at worse risk, I wasn't going to be easy to live with—ever again. I mean me and myself. Nor of course would I win the sympathy of the French police. That *salaud* of a *flic* could read in my face the way I felt about her. He knew I loved her. I knew he knew.

"Okay."

The officer gave a self-satisfied smile. "Just see what he wants," he said.

I took a pace forward, but he grabbed my arm and held me back.

"Your aim of course, Monsieur, must be to arrange for an exchange."

"Exchange?" I asked dumbly.

"You—for the girl. Naturally. She is of value, Monsieur. In terms of a hostage, I mean. She is an employee of the French State."

I gave him what must have been an odd look. I knew I was self-employed, a living insult to all centralized nation-states, but this was carrying discrimination too

186

far. Sure I wanted Sophie out of there, but the point was to be free with her.

"I'll see what I can do," I said, and made for the shaft down into the dank galleries of the mine.

As the stairwell disappeared behind me, I tried not to speculate. A yard inside the shot-away door the darkness closed in, and there was little chance of thinking of anything else except my immediate physical safety. Yet even so a sense of wonder, of disbelief in what I was doing came flooding back . . . like the sea into the mine at high tide.

Bozhe moy . . . I've never been a great believer in man's free will, but this looked suspiciously like an example of it. I could have said no . . . couldn't I? And I was thinking in Russian!

"Vladimir! There'll be a ladder in front of you. Be careful!"

Sophie's clear, calm but distant voice gave me courage.

I waited a second until my eyes got used to the black and felt around with my feet and hands. A handrail guided me to the top of a vertical shaft, then I leaned out over it. My feet began climbing down of their own accord. There was a kink to the left after four or five yards, then the shaft straightened out again. A flash-light beam shone up from what looked like a mile below, but was probably ten yards. It shone right in my face. I forced a smile.

"Merci! I'll be right down."

The sergeant-major kept the light on me as I clanged down rung after rung, the smell of the sea growing stronger as I descended. The walls of the shaft were streaked with rivulets.

"Where's the plutonium?"

That was all I could think of saying. My unconscious self had got into a panic about being cooped up down here with a canister of the stuff, even though it was Sophie I was supposed to be thinking of.

Sophie, standing in an alcove carved into the granite walls of a small chamber, a kind of resting place between shafts, pointed to her right. I saw the opening of the next shaft, not directly below the one leading up to the surface—presumably so that if you lost your grip near the top you didn't fetch up right down at sea level.

"Gone?" I said. "It's in the sea?"

She shook her head.

I followed the direction of her hand beyond the opening of the shaft. The canister was as far away as it could be. But still uncomfortably close, in the corner of the chamber, perhaps ten yards away.

"It doesn't look too happy there," I said.

"Tell that to him."

The sergeant-major, when I glanced at him, gave a deep sigh. It was out of character. I tried to get a better look at him, which wasn't easy considering he was still shining the flashlight more or less straight at me.

"Well?"

I looked from one to the other. Neither answered. The sea slurped and sucked somewhere down below. I shivered.

"Has he still got his *tac-tac?*" I said eventually, for something to say, seeking Sophie's eyes through the flashlight's beam.

"Cut the crap," said the sergeant-major.

"He's thinking," said Sophie. "Let him think."

I looked again toward Sophie. I made a face at her, trying to ask if she'd found any way out down through the old seams of the mine. Maybe the *flic* had been

188

talking out of the top of his *casquette*. She understood me and shook her head. The strands of her wet gold hair glinted at the edge of the halo that the sergeant-major was shedding around me, and the cashmere butterflies fanned their smudged pastel wings as she breathed gently in and out.

We both smiled, but unhappily.

"We investigated," she said softly. "No way. That is why he is thinking." She paused, saw the sergeant-major wasn't listening, and went on. "I can tell you now, Vladimir, we're all lucky to be alive. I wasn't bluffing about the danger of the cooling bath up there. I was in a panic that it could have been worse. If the dimensions had been different, if there'd been just a little more plutonium, it could have set off a real chain reaction."

"What do you mean?"

"Very high temperature. The water boiling instantly, flooding back in, boiling again. And each time a blue lightning flash. That's the Cerenkov effect. If you've seen it, you're dead. That's the really fatal radiation. Like that man saw in Colorado."

I swallowed hard. "I saw you ducking," I said.

"Reflex. But you, it would have been you who couldn't escape . . . I didn't *think* the mass was critical. But, *mon Dieu,* you cannot ever be sure in this kind of situation." She sighed.

The silence that followed seemed to bring the sergeant-major out of his reverie.

"Georges," he said at last. "Is he dead?"

"He smells of pine," I said, "but they may have to use the coffin for someone else. You'll see him again. If you play your cards right."

Was that the right way for me to play that card?

He seemed satisfied. Another pause followed.

Then: "You know why I want you down here, Ivan?"

"No. Three seems a crowd. Though it's a hell of a place to take a girl." I knew this was bad Hollywood style, but I was nervous. To be honest, frightened.

I put my hand against the wall and a little stream made its way down inside my sleeve. The wet penetrated the wool and I snatched my arm away as if some slimy beast had crawled in there.

"Because I want you to get me out of here alive," he said slowly.

"That's fine by me," I said. "How?"

"She'll tell you."

Sophie folded her arms to generate a bit more warmth and looked at me. "All I want to do is get this place decontaminated as fast as possible," she said, speaking in her fast, level French. "The sergeant-major can get nothing more out of this whole affair except his life. And he does not trust the *flics* up there. I do not blame him. He cannot stay here for much longer anyway. So it is just a question of how he gets out without getting shot. Preferably, from his point of view, without getting arrested. There are two ways of doing that. One is to use us as cover. One in front, one behind. But they have top-class marksmen. They can hit him if he shows them as much as one square centimeter, which one of us might just be tempted to help him expose when he isn't ready for it. And he knows it."

"Yes," I said, though the quiet menace in Sophie's voice was convincing enough. "The officer gave me a hint too. So the alternative is?"

It seemed odd discussing the situation like this in front of the sergeant-major. But he seemed beyond caring.

"You," said Sophie, "are now his negotiator. He will not let me go. He has told me that quite clearly. I am the only card he has. Okay. So if you do not mind climbing up and down that ladder . . . ."

"It'll keep me warm. What are his terms?"

This time Sophie looked squarely at the sergeant-major, who lowered the flashlight, stared at me, then at her.

"First of all, you and the girl come up with me," he growled. "They clear out of the tower, keep fifty meters away at all times. No discussions. Yes or no. And it has to be yes. Or I kill both of you and come out shooting."

"They won't say no as long as Mademoiselle Bonnissent comes up first and unharmed," I improvised. "They know as well as we all do there's no way out except up. Up and then out by the front door. Unless you fancy diving sixty feet onto the rocks and swimming to Guernsey in midwinter. That'd be madness, *if* that's what you're thinking. But I don't see how . . ."

"Shut up," said the sergeant-major. "That's not everything. The plutonium. That comes up with me."

"It'll kill you."

The sergeant-major said mockingly: "There's worse than that. I've seen the inside of a dryer. I know what that means."

"Think of it as a cooler," I said. "That has a more welcoming feel."

"Don't be clever, Bolcho. Tell 'em up there I'm in the market. I'll sell." He stopped, thought hard and then said, "The price is a boat. Sir Ronald's boat, in fact. They must bring the *St. George* round from Diélette. I'm sure they've found it by now."

I nodded.

"Right below the mine here. Tied up to the first

platform. Then left with the engine running. I want my brother put in, and in good condition. Then everyone clears right out. He's okay, you say?" Involuntarily he gave his own head a rub. "That old bastard . . . ."

"Georges was alive when I last saw him," I said. "Enough, I reckon, to show you he's not dead."

I realized I was talking like those doctors who examined Pinocchio—if he's not by some curious chance dead, then it's a sure sign he is alive; alternatively, if he happens to be dead . . . .

"What makes you think they won't just shoot you anyway?" I added, hoping to get off this subject.

"Because I won't give 'em a clear target," said the sergeant-major. "I'll keep control of the canister. They won't run the risk of hitting the plutonium. I'll keep it moving, keep dodging. You know what'll happen if they do?"

"I might be able to guess," I said. Then to Sophie: "Tell us."

"It probably wouldn't explode," she said evenly. "But it would spread the plutonium oxide powder around. Depends on how near anyone got, which way the wind is blowing and so on. But it would be deadly —inhaling a single particle is enough to kill."

"All right," I said. "I get the idea. You want me to go and fix all that up."

"Vladimir. You're forgetting one thing."

Sophie's voice was low but firm. "It's crazy to let him go up there with that canister." She glanced at the faint gleam of the container in the corner. "With your permission, *mon cher*, I suggest we call his bluff."

She was looking intently at the sergeant-major all the time she was speaking. His only reaction was a tightening of the muscles in his right hand, his finger tensing in the trigger guard of the submachine gun.

"Georges will not be helped," she went on. "At the moment he is just bruised. That is right, is it not?"

I nodded firmly.

"Traveling with an overheated can of plutonium for company," she went on, "that is an imbecilic way to cure his sore head. No one is going to do him any more damage up there. Georges did not even kill anyone that I know of. Leave him alone, sergeant-major. Do him a real service."

There was another of those long silences.

One thing at least we could be sure of. The sergeant-major had not prepared this scene. He had not thought things through this far. It was his opportunism against ours. The only advantage he had was that he was more desperate. We had a future to look forward to; he had one, too, of course, but in no way could it be anticipated with pleasure. I had the impression we had everything to gain if we just kept him talking.

"It won't work, will it?" I said. "You know that, sergeant-major, as well as I do."

He looked at me. I detected, or thought I detected, a glimmer of fear behind the hostility.

"This way you die," I continued inexorably. "You put the canister on board a small boat with your brother for any length of time and Georges gets radioactive. All he's got now is a bump on his head. Not to mention everyone else on board eventually getting contaminated. And a plutonium canister's worse protection than a person, whatever you say—a damn sight smaller than Sophie or me, and it can't cover you front and back. The closer you keep it to you to protect yourself the deadlier it is. Catch-22."

"Vladimir's right," Sophie said quietly.

"Then what in hell do I do?" the sergeant-major suddenly yelled. "You two are so fucking clever. How would you get out of here if you were me, *hein?*"

Suddenly his words choked in his throat. He was practically sobbing. His nerves were going.

"Ah well, let's see," I said coolly, hoping to give a further twist to the downward spiral. "I don't like the idea of being cornered down here like a sewer rat any more than you do. Well, the fact you shot Pierre Denis complicates things, gives me a touch of *Schadenfreude.*"

"Hein?"

"Nothing. I'm just trying to think. Sophie, love, is there any way out the back of the tower?"

"As far as I know, it is a sheer drop into the sea."

The sergeant-major nodded grimly.

"Right," I said, warming to the project. I pretended to be occupied with the intellectual challenge of seeing just how it was possible for him to get out of here alive, the real point being that if we could prove to him there really was no way out there was a chance he would simply give himself up. It seemed reasonable psychology to me.

"Free Guernsey Movement!" the sergeant-major said contemptuously, out of nowhere. "Funny Games for Madmen! That's what Georges called it. *Merde!* It was only when I saw, well, Georges too, that we'd get our hands on the stuff, that plutonium shit . . . it was a gift too good to turn down. Hisland's crazy. His head's got a split in it."

"What was he going to do with his plutonium?" I asked, playing along.

"Do? He hadn't a clue. No bloody idea. He changed his mind every day."

"I guessed as much. He couldn't have figured out for himself, for example, that Mackeson-Beadle and I were going to come over after him, that he could set old Godfrey up as a fall guy."

The sergeant-major nodded, but he wasn't listening.

"I have a feeling Ronnie Hisland didn't dream up this idea alone as you suggest. Hell, you said yourself he didn't know what he was going to do with the stuff in the end. But *you* did. Didn't you?"

The sergeant-major was still silent. He was thinking hard. Did he still have hope?

"I think you planted the idea in his head," I went on. "You saw you had a trained bunch of men, trained at his expense, and you knew you couldn't get him involved if you simply said you wanted to steal plutonium and ransom it for cash. So you planted other ideas in his mind to cover for your own . . . ."

"What the hell does it matter either way? He believed it."

"Okay. I couldn't care less if you built the bandwagon or just jumped on it. Besides, Ronnie will get his. Whether he was led by the nose or not."

"You might find some advantage," Sophie put in quietly, "in helping the police find the others. I mean the rest of the team at the hijack."

"*Merde!*" said the sergeant-major again, sounding more and more depressed. "I don't know myself where they are. When they hear what's happened to me and Georges, they'll skip it even further."

"Still, you must have some information which could. . . ."

"Let's finish with that," he snapped. "I said no deals."

"Pity we haven't got a hang-glider. That would stun

them out there if you got up to the top of the tower and took off."

"Or a friend with an egg-beater," said the sergeant-major with heavy sarcasm. "Cut the crap, Gull."

Yes, I hadn't thought of a helicopter.

"Well," I said, putting on the finishing touches, "it doesn't look too good, does it? The water below and the *flics* above. Caught between the devil and the deep blue sea."

The sergeant-major fixed his own glare on the plutonium canister, that silent witness to our life-and-death debate.

"That *merde!* I wish I'd never heard of that shit. Filthy, lousy . . . ."

He leaped up and ran to where it lay, raised his right foot and kicked the canister hard. It skidded across the damp rock floor and twirled on its axis, spinning a few feet from the rim of the shaft that descended to the water line.

"No!" Sophie screamed at him as he followed it across, ready to give it the *coup de grâce* and send it plunging down. She grabbed his arm.

"If it smashes on the rocks down there, the tide will take it and spread it for kilometers around. You will pollute millions . . . ."

The sergeant-major hesitated as her voice trailed off.

He stood, motionless, at the top of the shaft, poised. For an instant, I thought he was wondering whether to throw himself down instead of the plutonium. Then he shook his head and walked slowly back to where he had been sitting before. He slumped back against the wall and let his gun fall onto his thighs.

"*Merde! Merde!*"

He shivered as if he had just stared death in the face and pulled back.

In a few seconds I should be able to walk over and just take his gun . . . .

Then, strangely, just when I thought we had him beat, his mood began to change. It happened quite quickly. As we watched, his features tightened, his body seemed to swell to fit his clothes again. His hands grasped the gun with their previous martial grip. We had given something away.

"*Bien,*" he announced. His voice too had regained a good part of the assurance it had lost during the moments of despair.

"You heard what I want, Gull," he said, hitching up his pants with a firm pull. "Don't try all that psychology shit on me. Okay. I see my way now. So get up that fucking ladder and tell 'em. I want the boat round here, motor running, Georges in it and every *flic* out of the tower. Period. If they don't agree, I kill the girl. You, too, if you come back with a 'no.' As for the plutonium, I'll kick that into the sea."

He looked straight into my eyes. There was no trace of fear, no vestige of the whipped spaniel.

"They may not give a shit for you, even for mademoiselle here," he said. And he tossed his submachine gun jauntily from right hand to left. "But they sure won't let this stuff float out on the tide. Oh, no."

So up the greasy ladder I went. Just when I thought at first he'd given up the idea of negotiating—when I thought he was ready to hand himself over. Just when I was then congratulating myself on at least out-psyching the bastard, thinking that his insistence on having

197

me as his sole intermediary gave me some special power over him, some psychological leverage.

As soon as I surfaced, I noticed the throbbing whine of rotor blades over my head. Outside the white tower, I looked up. A French army chopper flounced its tail around like a skittish can-can dancer and settled prissily on the misty cliff-top, as if afraid to dirty its shoes in the mud. Nobody was taking any notice of me. All eyes were turned to the small figure which emerged immediately from the flung-open door, ducked instinctively but unnecessarily, then made for the most senior-looking policeman—my friend with the thin mustache—hand outstretched for shaking.

Though drifting fog made visibility poor, I recognized the hard, squat little figure of the minister of the interior himself, Monsieur Raymond Peyrac.

Peyrac wore his habitual sunglasses. His habitual dark blue overcoat with its beaver collar was more suited, however, to the climate.

On the ridge there was a long series of handshakes and embraces, after which Peyrac gave several brisk parallel strokes to his hair, slicking it straight back on his small round head. Then he led a train of acolytes, like ravens in black coats and turned-up collars, down off the cliff-top, away from me at first, soon emerging from the direction of Diélette at a crisp jog.

The minister wasted no time either when he came up to me.

"I have arrived to take charge. I understand you have been in the mine with the criminal. The first thing I need is a brief situation report omitting no substantive details."

I seemed to give the minister what he wanted because he nodded in a self-satisfied way at the end, as if his question had been so accurately put that it demanded just such a reply.

"The interests of the French State are clear," he said, enunciating ostentatiously so that a wide circle could hear him. Unlike the others, who seemed preoccupied by keeping their shoes out of the puddles and slurry, Peyrac had the capacity to concentrate totally on the matter in hand. The only one to match his single-minded intentness was the police officer with the patrolman's mustache who stood at permanent attention at the minister's left. "France demands," the minister continued, "that her shores—and her people—remain unpolluted. My first duty therefore is to ensure that the plutonium remains here, at the Flamanville mine, that it remains intact in its container. The first plutonium theft to occur in France is scandalous enough. For the crime to result in poison being spread, an example being set to criminals in other countries, is unthinkable." He turned to his left. "I appoint you, Monsieur le Commandant, as the senior officer of police present, you who are a proud member of the Compagnie Républicaine de Sécurité directly under my control, to negotiate for the safe return of the plutonium. I wish you first . . . ."

"One moment, Monsieur le Ministre. The sergeant-major . . . the criminal, has told me specifically that he wishes *me* to act as negotiator," I said, stepping forward.

"The orders I have given are clear," snapped Peyrac. "I have heard your report, Monsieur Gull" (he even remembered my name) "with interest. But now it really is time for the public authorities to take command of the situation."

"He'll never accept a member of the CRS down there. He told me as much. Besides, you're forgetting one thing, Monsieur le Ministre, there's not just plutonium with him down there, there's also a woman."

A minion stepped forward.

"The minister has not . . ."

But his words were drowned by the roar of another helicopter that came over the cliff edge, circled the white tower dangerously low and close, it seemed to me, and whirled around toward the cliff and back into the fog. I thought for a moment we were being visited by the President himself, anxious perhaps for a share of the credit if things went well, but the marking on the silver chopper was loud and clear: TIME-LIFE INC. Camera lenses bristled from the windows like the barrels of anti-tank guns. Ronnie Hisland wasn't so far wrong, I thought to myself. The whole world *is* going to know, and damn soon, about his caper. Pity he can't enjoy the show.

Raymond Peyrac quickly took the policeman's arm and ushered him in the direction of the mineshaft.

"The honor of France . . ." I heard him mutter, as the *flic,* cradling a *mitraillette* and issuing soft orders to be well covered, stepped forward and peered down the black hole.

I knew it was useless. But let them find it out the hard way.

"Holà!"

Silence greeted the policeman's first cry.

"Holà! You! Leave the plutonium where it is and come out with the girl. We will not shoot."

Silence.

He beckoned me over to him and asked in a stage whisper, "Any chance of our hitting the guy from up here?"

"No," I said firmly. "The shaft doesn't even go down

in a straight line. Besides, Sophie . . . ."

"Will he shoot?"

"I think so. His nerves aren't as steady as they might be. The plutonium, for instance, damn near went into the sea already. I suggest—"

"Thank you, Monsieur." He waved me away, then cupped his hand around his mouth and shouted again down the shaft. "I am coming in one minute. Do not shoot. In one minute. I am coming unarmed."

The policeman placed his submachine gun carefully on the damp concrete steps. Immediately afterward he undid the top buttons of his black uniform jacket and made a few practice swoops at the handgun that nestled in his armpit.

I shook my head, but kept quiet, hoping that Sophie would be okay.

Ostentatiously counting the seconds on his large wristwatch, the policeman waited out the minute. The minister, at the back of the white tower, was frowning.

One minute passed.

"*Holà!* I am coming. I intend only to—"

A shot zinged up from the mineshaft.

The *flic* jumped back; then glanced around shamefacedly at the minister.

"I think maybe I . . ." I began.

"Monsieur Gull," the minister interrupted at once, stepping forward smartly like a volunteer from the ranks and smiling icily. I prefered his habitual poker face. "Clearly the man below is unreasonable. You, however, maintain that he is prepared to talk—if not to reason—with yourself. I must take exceptional circumstances into account. Besides, the lives of officers . . . ."

"Of the French State are precious. I know."

"Monsieur Gull," he continued unsmiling. "You are on French territory. It is your duty therefore to comply with the laws of France and to obey all orders given you by the legally appointed authorities." He paused and looked into my eyes through his dark glasses, knowing that I could read nothing in his own. Drops of moisture quivered on the sleek fur of his coat collar. "The man down there is dangerous. He is holding the whole of France to ransom. He possesses one of the world's most deadly substances. He . . . yes, I anticipate your words, Monsieur Gull. He is also holding as hostage an employee of the French State. Every effort must be made. In the circumstances, you must step forward. You must go down and reason with the man. You must persuade him that for reasons of State—"

"I know what must be done, Monsieur le Ministre," I said, losing patience. "But it may take time. And it will certainly take patience, and restraint. The criminal is likely to make demands. There will be certain . . . negotiations. I understand France is waiting for results. So is the whole world." I glanced up at the sky, where the noise of the news helicopter was waxing and waning in the thick fog. "But for me human life is more important than any *raison d'état.* Even a single human life, illogical as I know that proposition sounds now. I only promise to do what I can."

Quite a pretty speech, I thought, under the circumstances. Worthy of the Chamber of Deputies. Raymond Peyrac showed no enthusiasm for it, however, though he also desisted from giving it the bird.

"As for the terms that you claim he mentioned, Monsieur Gull," he continued with his perfectly even, clipped, baritone voice. "As for his so-called terms, one thing is paramount: the plutonium stays where it is. But he can have the boat. He can even have my helicopter, if he thinks of it."

"And his brother?"

"Tell the man that his brother is too sick. He has gone to hospital."

"Is that true?"

"What is that to you, Monsieur Gull? I will tell you what you need to know."

That sounded like real confidence in a mediator.

I turned to the chief of police. "Do you think you can actually avoid shooting if the sergeant-major comes up with Sophie and me screening him, with or without the plutonium?"

"My men are well trained," he replied, bristling. "They will do nothing without my orders. But let's get that point cleared up first—no plutonium. If we see a clear shot, we'll shoot past you to kill. You just be good hostages."

With that cheerful advice ringing in my ears, I made my way down again, shouting I was coming to make sure the sergeant-major knew it was me. The responsibility was becoming heavier each minute. My heart was pounding. At least my body temperature was being kept up by all the exercise. The air in the shaft was barely above freezing.

The sergeant-major was waiting for me impatiently.

"All set up?"

"Now just wait," I said, catching my breath. "There's a bit of negotiating to do first. That's why I got the job, remember? Also, Peyrac's up there."

"The Minister?"

The sergeant-major's face muscles tightened as his expression changed from one of self-importance to anxiety.

I told him their position. I recounted what they had said up there about Georges, the boat, us . . . and the plutonium. I was puzzled myself as to what the sergeant-major's plans were exactly—how the hell did he plan to get to the boat, for instance?—but one step at a time.

He thought for a good two minutes before replying.

"Tell them this, Vladimir. The plutonium comes up with me. Otherwise no deal. So does *Mademoiselle*. You I couldn't give a shit about. Neither could they."

He laughed for the first time since he'd entered the mineshaft. It wasn't a joke I appreciated.

"And I want Georges in the boat, hospital or no hospital. *Entendu?* He shot one of them, so I want him with me. And the motor running. No compromises. No *hics*. Okay?"

"And now you want me to get up there and tell them? They'll never let you take the plutonium. Wouldn't it be better if—?"

"*Écrase*, Gull! Just move. And bring me down some rope. One coil. Leave the other."

"Okay."

I turned to Sophie with a questioning look.

She merely nodded cheerlessly. Exhaustion and cold were catching up with her.

"Tell them to hurry, Vladimir," she added after a second's thought. "Too long down here with that thing, even at this distance,"—she glanced at the canister— "and it all becomes academic."

I scrambled up the ladder yet again. This time they were waiting for me with more attention, except that mine was distracted by a scuffle that was going on along the path leading to Diélette. About six cameramen were being wrestled unceremoniously out of sight by a group of vizored CRS. One camera went flying and broke on the rocky ground. The foggy air filled with angry shouts.

I looked around.

"Where's the minister?"

The senior police officer took me by the elbow. "Well?"

"Where's the minister?" I repeated.

The chief *flic* pointed up to the cliff. "At his helicopter. He wishes to maintain constant radio communication with Paris. Well?"

I went over the sergeant-major's demands.

"Wait."

I waited.

One voice caught my attention in the crowd. I couldn't see the man involved, but it was obviously that of an Interior Ministry minion, one of the ravens. He was saying something I thought ominous. The offer of the minister's helicopter, he briefed the officers, was just a public relations gesture. The minister, he told them, had ordered the sergeant-major to be shot before he could ever dirty the chopper with his muddy boots. All the angles of fire had been studied. I caught the words: "the man must be taken at any price, as an example to the world of French determination."

Then the officer returned. He was surprisingly cooperative. I was expecting a row.

"We agree," he said promptly. "The boat is on its way round now. Georges is here. We'll put him aboard, but he's still unconscious. The plutonium, however, *has* to stay here at the mine. But it can come back up the shaft. We agree to that now. Under no circumstances, however, will we permit the criminal to take the canister aboard the boat. Or the helicopter, if he should choose that option. To prevent that, I am prepared to shoot him, the girl, you too. Even at the risk too of contaminating the area. Here at least the pollution can be contained. If he takes it . . . the whole nation is at risk."

I glanced up toward the official helicopter on top of the cliff. The fog cleared briefly as I did so. The minister was revealed addressing a crowd of representatives of the world's press, not communicating with Paris. Notebooks waved all around him, microphones were pressed toward his lips, flashbulbs popped dully. Ah, well, he's doing his duty, I thought, in his way.

Then I tidied up the last details with the police officer and drew in a deep breath.

Down below, in the mine, I was just as surprised that the sergeant-major agreed readily to the condition that the plutonium shouldn't leave the mine area as I had been over the minister's concession that it could come up the shaft.

"I knew they'd never agree to me keeping that *merde*," he said. "Not Peyrac anyway. This way I choose *when* to give it up. How is the fog up there?"

"Thicker than ever. Too thick for trying to get out by chopper, I'd say."

The sergeant-major didn't go for it, but merely nodded absentmindedly, taking the rope I offered him, then tied one end of the coil into a slip knot. He seemed to have his own plans worked out precisely, and they involved a boat, not a helicopter.

Then he put the noose around the canister and pulled it tight. He paid out three yards of rope, then announced: "Like this no one gets dirty." He peered up the shaft. "*Allez!* Vladimir first. Mademoiselle, you next. And you pull this up after you. I'll come last. And don't forget I'm a trained soldier. I can fire a gun and climb a ladder at the same time."

There was still no chance to talk to Sophie. I could see she was weighing up the possibilities on her own. But it would have been good to coordinate plans.

"*Allez!*"

I began what I hoped was the last climb up the damn ladder. Sophie followed, her hands grabbing the rungs as soon as my feet left them. The sergeant-major had tied the rope around her waist with the knot behind her so she could not untie it quickly. The ends hung down the shaft behind her, one of them attached to the canister that bounced and banged like a can attached to a cat's tail . . . or a piece of debris behind a newlyweds' car.

At last I put my head over the top and looked up the stairwell.

The sergeant-major yelled behind me, "They up there, Vladimir? They've cleared out?"

"They've gone," I yelled, loud enough to be heard by the officer standing by the silo watching me through the open doorway, holding a pistol. He drew back out of sight.

This was the point at which I really began to feel frightened. Now I was caught between two devious, trigger-happy men, neither of whom put my life high on their list of priorities. Thank God Sophie was sticking close behind.

"Hold it there!"

The sergeant-major climbed up into the stairwell and looked over the top, like a doughboy in a trench. He turned to Sophie. "Leave the canister hanging. Don't untie the rope from your waist till I give the order. Keep right up here in view and don't move. Try to stop what I'm going to do and I'll drop you. Russkoff too."

He was right back in his old form.

The sergeant-major scrambled out of the stairwell like a crab, making quickly for the stores piled in a protected corner. From his new vantage point he searched around for any view of a *flic.* But they hadn't tried to trick him. So far.

He found what he wanted. A new coil of rope. He put it over his head like a Mexican bandit's bandolier. Then, keeping to cover behind pillars and concrete slabs and other debris, he zigzagged across to the north wall of the white tower.

"Where's the boat?" he yelled.

"Ready and waiting," came a voice from below.

Up from below? Of course, the chute. For God's sake, *that* was his way out.

"Anybody stays on board, they get shot," shouted the sergeant-major. "Georges! You there?"

"He's there. But he's not talking," came back the same voice as before. "His jaw is bandaged."

"That better be the truth," the sergeant-major replied, less energetically, not caring if they heard him. He was already working at a strong knot, tying the end of the rope to a solid stanchion about a yard in from the exit of the chute. He tugged it and was satisfied.

"Okay," he shouted. "Can you still hear me out there?"

"I can hear you." That was the officer's voice. "If you try to take that canister of plutonium on the boat, we will shoot and to hell with the risk. *Compris?*"

"The plutonium stays tied to the girl," he yelled back into the fog. "If you shoot before I get to the boat, I shoot her and the canister. She'll be in my sight all the time. If you want to confirm, ask her."

"That's true," Sophie shouted. Then to me with a wan smile, "It's like taking a cat for a walk on a lead."

"A wild cat," I said, laughing, trying to ease her tenseness . . . as well as my own.

"Okay," said the sergeant-major, his eyes gleaming with the ecstasy of action. Down there in the mineshaft he had weakened almost to the point of despair. Up here, pitting himself mentally and physically against a hugely superior opposition, he was the hero, justifying his own image of himself. "It's out and down. I'll tell you just how I want it done. Ivan first. Get to the beach and wait. Mademoiselle slings out the canister, then she follows. Go down slowly. I'll be right behind you, *ma cocotte*. If they try to drop me, I'll fall right on you. Even if I don't get a shot in first. That plutonium'll burst like a grenade if it hits the rocks or the surf. They won't risk that. Don't either one of you communicate with the *flics*. Don't answer their questions. Nothing. When we're all down, I'll give you new orders. *Allez!*"

And he hurled the heavy coil of blue-and-white nylon rope out through the chute down to the rocks sixty feet below.

MY ARMS were already aching, stiff from the business with the ladder. It was all I could do to support myself on the thin, swaying rope. Luckily, I'd had to do it once before, out of a window in Italy. What kept me going was the canister of plutonium gyrating down three or four yards above my head. I didn't even try to see where the police were. It would have been a waste of effort because I dropped at once below the level of a granite wall that plunged, parallel to my own descent, directly onto the seaweed-covered rocks. Besides, anything not in close-up was invisible in the fog. Just like back on the cliff face, that was a hell of an advantage for someone prone to vertigo.

So long as the *flics* didn't try shooting . . . .

Shit! The rope began burning my palms and the soft fleshy insides of my fingers. It was too damn thin! The pain seared my hands and I half let go. My body dropped alarmingly. The pain was even worse when I held on. But it was that or death. Oh Christ! Tears spurted into my eyes from the pain. My muscles sent out spasm-messages to my brain . . . stop! I couldn't. Hand over hand I dropped down the rope. I tried to slow down, to let my feet or my ankles take the strain.

"Not so bloody fast," I yelled up to Sophie.

God, she was better adapted for these gymnastics than I was.

Three quarters of the way down, I spotted the boat . . . the magnificent *St. George,* not its little yellow dinghy I'd seen before in Diélette harbor but the real thing, even more impressive and powerful than Mackeson-Beadle's cabin cruiser. Upstaging his rival as usual. Moored fore and aft to the legs of the pylon, the motor yacht was rolling in the swell, its bow striking and scraping the rusty iron and the concrete platform in which the legs were set. There were only three fenders over the side, and the yellow paintwork of the boat was streaked with brown. Its engine was throbbing, basso profundo.

The boat provided the mental distraction I needed. Just when the pain came flooding back, my feet touched slime. I stumbled, falling and scrambling out of the way of the canister as it too bounced on the rocks right after me. All around was debris from the burnt-out Simca, the human remains so thoroughly incinerated that I couldn't, thank God, distinguish them from the car's.

I collapsed on a bed of seaweed, waving my hands in a desperate attempt to cool the burns.

Sophie, dangling on the end of the rope, kicked her feet up like a child on a swing and propelled herself clear of the danger.

The sergeant-major skillfully kept the rope in his ankles and cradled the submachine gun, keeping it pointed at us, steady as a rock. His was the real commando performance.

"Okay," he said, still poised over us. He was smiling. "Keep your pet on the leash for the next stage. Don't worry. I know the quarantine regulations. It won't come aboard."

Then he skewed off the rope at an angle, twisted and turned to face us, teeth gleaming, all in one sinuous movement like Douglas Fairbanks—*père et fils.*

"Bolcho! *Allez, 'op!* Up in the boat. Wait for me there."

I picked my way down to the edge of the sea. The icy water grabbed my ankles like a vise. I shouted in renewed pain.

"Get on in," said the sergeant-major. "It's lovely."

But how?

Once again it was like that Hugo novel *'Ninety-three,* the scene of the runaway cannon charging about the lurching hold of the *Claymore* like a loose bull, crushing the men who tried to restrain it. Here it was the whole boat that threatened to crush me. Viewed from above, the big cabin cruiser had looked securely enough moored, but close up it was obvious how slack the ropes were. The noise of surf and the scraping and crashing of boat against pylon was awful. Still, if that military bastard was going to play Douglas Fairbanks, I could have a try at Errol Flynn. I waited till the bow lurched forward on a wave and grabbed the head line as it went slack—to hell with the hands, what was a few more seconds of pain now? Then, with the boat in retreat, I snapped myself up on the wet line as it tautened, crawled up it upside down like a monkey and wrapped my feet gratefully around the chrome railing at the bow. Another tug and twist and I was lying exhausted and soaked in spray and sweat on the polished planks of the *St. George.*

"Hey! The ladder! Russkoff, let down the ladder!"

I put my head over the side. The sergeant-major was below me, the waves sucking at his shins. He didn't seem to mind the cold.

Yes, there was a ladder. It just needed a couple of catches undoing, and it would slip down the side of the boat. But should I do it? The sergeant-major couldn't get aboard without it. Not without giving me the chance to knock him senseless while he did his own circus act up the rope.

I hesitated but he read my mind.

"Do it, Bolcho, or I'll blow the girl's brains out. Move!"

What were those *flics* doing up there? Couldn't they get a shot in now? He was three or four yards away from the plutonium, two from Sophie who was still leading the can around like her pet pussycat. I looked up into the fog. If I couldn't see them, how the hell could they see us? And if they couldn't get a sure shot, they'd never risk it with Sophie and the plutonium anywhere near, not when even a ricochet could unloose the deadly dust over us . . . and them too.

The ladder rumbled down the hull of the *St. George.* The last rung splashed into the sea.

Now, was he going to leave Sophie or take her, and with or without the attached canister? How far *had* he worked all this out?

An ugly thought occurred to me. They hadn't had time to booby-trap the boat, had they? Thinking maybe he'd take off in it alone?

The big cabin cruiser was bobbing like a cork in the breaking surf, shuddering each time it struck the pylon. I was already feeling seasick. Lucky Georges, unconscious . . . in the cabin, I guessed. The boat lurched forward again, almost caught the sergeant-major, veered to his left. He backed higher up on the rocks.

Sophie was watching us intently, that radioactive pet of hers still trailing behind her. The rope coiled around her waist passed through her hands, then snaked out to the plutonium canister lying two yards behind her in a cleft between two small rocks. The metal reflected spots of spray.

She stood crouched, like a hammer thrower at the Olympic games.

A hammer . . . !

Suddenly I understood.

"I'll give you a hand up!" I shouted at the sergeant-major.

"Get back, Ivan," he yelled against the crashing of the surf. "I come up alone."

A wave hit the boat so that its bow end reared in the air. I exaggerated its effect and clutched at the rail . . . placing myself just above the ladder. The sergeant-major rose with the sea, his feet on the bottom rung.

As the boat dived back, thumping the pylon, Sophie saw her chance. Her hand snaked down the rope. In a single jerk she swung the seven-and-a-half-pound canister straight at the sergeant-major.

It slammed into his left kidney. She jerked again, pulling it back from over the sea on the end of its tether, and let it tamely down onto the rocks. It was safe. But the sergeant-major screamed with pain and fury. His head whipped around. The gun came up, cradled for firing in his right arm.

I jumped. My 170 pounds crunched down on his shoulders.

His left hand, the one gripping the ladder, flew outward. His body corkscrewed, toppled, fell. We landed in the sea together. A wave smashed over our heads. I thought only of the gun. So did he. At least I had one end of it. That was enough.

Just enough. I was losing my grip as we thrashed together in the icy surf when Sophie, free of the rope, threw herself in.

She had just time to get an armlock on the sergeant-major's head before all three of us went under. I ducked down, picked up a heavy, slippery stone and lifted it, waiting for him to surface. But a crest of surf knocked me off balance. I yelled in frustration as I fell sideways. The stone slipped from my hands and fell harmlessly back.

I floundered back into action at once, as the sergeant-major and Sophie surfaced together, spluttering. I thumped him with as solid a left and a right as I could, left to the solar plexus, right to the balls. He opened his mouth to scream. Water poured in. He flailed back, choking. One blow caught me on my forehead, but I felt nothing. I grabbed Sophie's hand and pulled her away from him. He sprang forward at me, but a wave caught him and flung him backward and under water again. I jumped on him—on where he had been. But the sea had dragged him to the right. Into Sophie! Shit! I picked up another rock.

How long this chaotic battle—almost unseemly, viewed from above—would have gone on, God alone knew. No one was being very effective. The surf made sure of that. But someone heard our yelling. We were still in a tangle, mermaid and mermen stranded too close to shore and desperately flapping back in, when the Figures in black—themselves scarcely human in visors and shiny boots—came tumbling in and grabbed hold of the sergeant-major.

I staggered to my feet and spouted like a whale.

Sophie clambered to my side and knelt in the surf. She began to laugh hysterically with relief, with cold, with the strain on her muscles and her mind.

"They're safe," she shouted, "they're safe! All my little pussycats are safe!"

I laughed, took her in my arms, hugged her, kissed her, pressed my lips to her salty face. A wave broke us apart. Burly men in uniforms picked us separately out of the water.

As I hit the stretcher, I was aware of a zoom lens pointing down at my face.

"Don't look right at the camera . . . uh-huh, give us brave smile . . . great!"

Don Gaffney took his eye from the viewfinder and winked.

"Okay," he said. "It's in the can. I left the *Time* magazine guy standing at the post. But don't worry, Vladimir. You'll still make the cover."